He couldn't hav

Mary leaned back against the railing, admiring the twinkling stars against a blue velvet sky as he talked. She loved the way Nelson's voice sang across her heartstrings, and if he wanted to stand there forever and talk, she'd be content to listen that long.

A few moments of silence passed before he emitted a silent chuckle and turned to her. "You know, lately I was starting to think you were avoiding us. Or to be more precise, avoiding me."

The fine hairs on her arms prickled, and the breeze suddenly felt chilly.

"Was I wrong?"

Mary could find no reason to hide the truth. He'd find out soon enough, anyway. She lowered her gaze and shook her head.

"So, which was it then? The family or me?"

"Both."

He released a sudden rush of breath, and his shoulders flattened.

"But not for reason you think."

SALLY LAITY Having successfully written several novels, including a coauthored series for Tyndale, several Barbour novellas, and numerous Heartsongs, this author's favorite thing these days is counseling new authors via the Internet. Sally always loved to write, and after her four children were grown, she took college writing courses and attended Christian writing conferences. She has written both historical and contemporary romances, and considers it a joy to know that the Lord can touch other hearts through her stories. She makes her home in Bakersfield, California, with her husband and enjoys being a grandma.

Books by Sally Laity

Don't miss out on any of our super romances. Write to us at the following address for information on our newest releases and club membership.

Heartsong Presents Readers' Service
PO Box 719
Uhrichsville, OH 44683

Remnant of Forgiveness

Sally Laity

Heartsong Presents

To Marjorie Burgess, a shining star, a loving heart, an inspiration to us all, this book is lovingly dedicated. Her unwavering faith and courageous hope have been a true reflection of our Lord Jesus Christ. Thank you, Margie.

Special thanks to Dianna Crawford and Andrea Boeshaar. May God bless you always.

A note from the author:
I love to hear from my readers! You may correspond with me by writing:

Sally Laity
Author Relations
PO Box 719
Uhrichsville, OH 44683

ISBN 1-58660-170-9

REMNANT OF FORGIVENESS

All Scripture quotations, unless otherwise noted, are taken from the King James Version of the Bible.

Cover illustration by Victoria Lisi and Julius.

PRINTED IN THE U.S.A.

prologue

Poland, 1945

A chilly spring wind wailed across the ashes of Warsaw, as if mourning the loss of the once proud capital's soul. Only the multistoried Polonia Hotel and a few other buildings remained unscathed—the ones the German armies had required for headquarters or troop barracks. The rest had been bombed or gutted by fire. Gone were the tree-lined streets and magnificent landmarks renowned throughout Europe. The main marketplace, the *Rynek*, lay in rubble. Twisted and blackened ruins marked the demise of the formerly luxurious railroad station. Even the Blue Palace, frequented in bygone days by pianist and former premier of Poland, Jan Ignacy Paderewski, had been reduced to waste. Block by block, building by building, the bombs, cannons, and fires of the methodical and relentless Nazi destruction had spared nothing, not even cathedrals or hospitals. The latter, they had torched while beds and corridors still teemed with helpless, trapped patients. The smoky pall of long-dead fires still lingered in the air, along with the sickeningly sweet odor of burned human flesh.

It is all as Josep told us, Marie Therese conceded bitterly. *Warszawa is dead.* Having learned to hold her emotions inside, she could not even speak for the heaviness that pressed upon her spirit as the young man affiliated with the Polish Relief Organization drove her and her Jewish friend, Rahel Dubinsky, along a crater-pocked street.

In this city, which used to bustle with streetcars and happy

5

children, they passed not even one automobile, only horse-drawn carts or bicycle-propelled pushcarts. What little trading still took place occurred on street corners, by ragged people in crudely constructed wooden shacks. Girls in Polish uniforms directed traffic, assisted by Red Army soldiers, and additional Soviet troops patrolled the city.

But most heartbreaking of all was the sight of the one-legged children, in nauseating numbers, hobbling about on such sticks as they could find, silently holding out grubby hands to passersby. Hatred for the German forces and their maniacal leader who had committed suicide to save himself from the world's retribution rose like bile in Marie's throat.

The depth of the rubble at *Stare Miastro,* the oldest section of town, forced Josep Klimek to park his rickety vehicle, and Marie and Rahel got out.

The faint drone of motors drifted toward them on the breeze, and Marie raised her gaze off into the distance, where a hand-ful of battered trucks carted away loads of debris. Except for the absence of that distinctive, abrasive squeaking, the sound seemed reminiscent of the Nazi tanks which had rumbled through the city six years ago, rendering an end to her peace-ful and idyllic life as the daughter of a professor and a French-born mother. . .a life that would never again be the same, once her father had spoken out against Adolf Hitler.

And it was even worse for her friend, Rahel.

Even before the German occupation, anti-Semitism had been strong in Warsaw. But nothing could have prepared the girls for the sight of the Ghetto, where Rahel, her family, and the rest of the Jewish population had been imprisoned behind barbed wire, enduring starvation and disease before their ultimate liquidation at Nazi death camps. The two could only stare in open-mouthed horror at the four square miles which had been utterly pulverized by the German army.

It broke what was left of Marie's heart to see tears roll from

Rahel's sunken brown eyes and down her sallow cheeks, making dark splotches on the faded coat. "Nothing is left," the devastated girl cried, her expressive face contorted with grief. "Nothing. I cannot even tell where Papa's shop used to be."

Marie put an empathetic arm around her friend's gaunt shoulders. Small comfort, but she had nothing else to offer.

"I had hoped to spare you," Josep reminded. The bearlike young man who had befriended the girls since they'd come back to Warsaw returned to the truck and waited for them to join him inside. Then he restarted the engine and inched forward again, steering around huge craters and the debris in their path to head out of the city, his truck bed packed with supplies for a village to the north.

"You are still positive I am to let you out in the middle of nowhere?" he asked a few minutes later. "Such a foolish scheme I cannot condone." He wagged his head, a shapeless charcoal felt hat shadowing the glower on a ruddy face lined beyond his thirty years.

Rahel stared straight ahead. "I am positive. I will tell you where."

"But two young women alone—even dressed like boys! It is folly." He cut them an incredulous scowl. "The Russian soldiers are worse than the Nazis. They are not so disciplined, and for women or young girls they have no respect at all. Right across the river, on the *Praga* side, they are shipping trainloads of Polish refugees to slave camps in Siberia. My head Ania will have if harm comes to either of you."

"Do not worry," came Rahel's calm assurance. "We will be careful. There are places to hide. We will watch for your return."

Marie Therese held her silence. Since their release from the concentration camp, Rahel had hinted of a secret she had harbored throughout their captivity. But she had yet to disclose the particulars.

The two of them had been through so much—even after Ravensbruck had been liberated. The majority of the freed Polish captives begged to return to their homeland to see what, if anything, remained of farms, businesses, or relatives of whom they'd received no word in months. Thanks to the efforts of the brave souls sympathetic to their cause, small groups of refugees were shepherded by night through Russian-occupied Eastern Germany, a harrowing journey none of them would likely forget.

When the pathetic lot finally gained the Polish border, the Polish Red Cross and other relief organizations took over. Among them were Josep Klimek and his wife, Ania, two more individuals doing the work of angels. The couple took Marie and Rahel into their care. For today's venture, they had even supplied the girls with men's clothing so they would more easily blend in with other workers around Warsaw. Hunching deeper into the scratchy jacket she wore, Marie drew a troubled breath and let her mind drift to the past as the truck wheezed and coughed its way up a lengthy rise.

Barely nineteen, it seemed a lifetime ago that she'd been a giggly schoolgirl in uniform, walking home from classes with her brothers and younger sister, blushing whenever a handsome boy glanced in her direction. As the daughter of a prominent college professor, she had traveled in far different circles from Rahel's, and would never have been allowed to associate with someone of the Jewish faith. Now this young, painfully thin woman was her only friend in the world. Like a sister. Both of them, along with a number of other naturally attractive and appealing young women, had been dispersed to various locations in Poland and Germany for the private entertainment of the Nazi officers.

Her and Rahel's destination had been Ravensbruck, the infamous German extermination camp.

Strange, how such a horrendous place could create an incredibly strong bond between individuals forced to suffer the unspeakable shame and agonies they had endured.

But what would become of them now? They could never return to the innocence of their lost youth.

Pondering her hollow future, Marie Therese almost envied the emaciated souls who'd met their end in the gas chambers. No amount of years would ever completely banish the memory of that squat, square concrete building smack in the middle of the grounds, the thin acrid vapor rising in a constant stream from its huge smokestack. Nor would she forget the horrendous, hellish sounds which emanated day and night from the punishment barracks, the lice and fleas, the constant gnawing hunger. Or parading naked before the snickering SS guards to the icy showers and humiliating medical examinations. . .and worse.

So much worse. . .

As the truck bumped and lurched over the unpaved country road, Marie deliberately forced her thoughts away from the horror to concentrate on the single good element of that despicable camp: an older Dutch spinster with the unlikely name of Corrie ten Boom. With a small Bible she and her sweet, frail, even older sister Betsie had somehow managed to smuggle past the guards, the dear woman had instilled a measure of hope to the wretched captives amassed in flea-infested Barracks 28.

Every night until lights-out, the pair would take turns reading Scripture passages. Some were familiar to Marie Therese. But what struck her most was the way Corrie spoke *of* God and *to* Him—as if He were her very closest Friend. Her words, spoken in Dutch, had to be translated by other women to be understood by the different nationalities. Marie surmised that somewhere along the line from Dutch to German, and then on to French, Russian, Polish, and Czech, the original thoughts acquired a far-too-lofty idealism that couldn't possibly be taken literally.

Nevertheless, in the cold dark of night, as the searchlight swept in regular intervals over the barracks walls, sending flashes of thin light through the rag-stuffed broken windows, those very promises brought an inner warmth to Marie beyond any the threadbare blankets provided to her body. And a hope that at least some of what Corrie had related was true.

Someday, somehow, she would obtain a Bible and search things out for herself. But for now she could only struggle to follow the older woman's admonition to dwell on thoughts of a loving God rather than on cruelty and hatred, however impossible that seemed at times. A ragged sigh came from deep inside.

"Here!" Rahel declared with force. "Stop."

Josep stomped on the worn brakes, and the old truck lumbered to a halt.

Marie Therese peered at the open, rolling countryside dotted here and there by woods. Traces of new green had begun to soften the stark winter-bare bushes and trees framing the fertile farmland. But the absence of freshly plowed furrows made the fields appear lonely and desolate, like a canvas waiting to be painted.

Rahel's bony elbow jabbed Marie's ribs, urging her to quit gawking and get out. "Do not forget the shovel," the dark-eyed girl reminded her.

Marie Therese nodded and opened the door, stepping down from the running board. From the truck bed she retrieved one of two digging tools Josep always carried with him. Rahel claimed the other.

"I'm going on now," he called to them, "to deliver these goods. In two hours I should be back. Maybe a little longer. Be careful. Keep your eyes peeled. Russian convoys come through all the time to plunder whatever is left from the towns and villages," he added grimly.

"We will be careful."

At her friend's confident statement, Marie gave a dubious smile and a nod to their benefactor and watched after the lorry as it chug-chugged over the next rise and vanished from sight, leaving a silence broken only by the sighing wind.

Marie turned to see her friend already well on her way toward an irregular grove of trees some distance away, the oversized tan coat flapping with each step. She only hoped the two of them did appear to be men, just in case. Tugging her hat more snugly over her hair, she hastened to catch up. "Where are we going?"

"Not far."

A stand of trees rose up from a spot where the contour of the land hid the road from view. Approaching the grove, the Jewish girl slowed, her dark eyes focusing on one tree in particular, studying the gnarled roots, its position among others. Then a corner of her lips curved in a tiny smile. "We will dig here." She jabbed the pointed end of her shovel into ground moist from recent rains, stepping on the dull side to add her weight.

Marie Therese followed suit, amazed to find herself quickly winded by the uncustomary exertion.

When they'd dug about a foot down, Rahel's shovel struck metal. "Ah!" She fell to her knees and sat back on the heels of her too big shoes, a satisfied smile adding a sparkle to her wide-set eyes. "Just where we left it, Papa, Aron, and I." She brushed aside the remaining layer of soil, revealing an object flat and round.

"What is it?" Marie panted, leaning on the handle of her own mud-caked shovel to catch her breath.

"Our future, yours and mine." Grasping what turned out to be the edge of a milk can lid, Rahel gave a mighty yank, but to no avail. "You must help. Take hold of the other side."

Marie sank down and added all the strength she possessed,

grunting and tugging along with Rahel. On the third try, it popped open with a loud squeak of protest and clunked to the ground.

Rahel reached inside the hollow interior of the buried container and withdrew a cotton sack, dumping out its contents.

Marie stared incredulously at more jewelry, loose gems, and *zluty,* Polish money, than she had ever seen at one time in her life.

"Papa was a wise man," Rahel explained, gathering the items and stuffing them back inside the bag. "He saw this war coming well in advance, knew that deep trouble would come upon our country. One day he brought our family here—for a picnic, we thought. But once we had eaten the food in the basket, he and Aron buried our savings at the base of this tree, in case we survived whatever was ahead." She paused, her chin trembling. "I. . .never imagined I would be the only one left to come back to reclaim it. Mama, Papa, my four brothers. . ." She met Marie's gaze through a sheen of tears.

It was the most the young Jewess had ever said at one time since their months of enforced silence. Reminded of her own wrenching loss, Marie Therese leaned close and hugged her hard, struggling to contain the anguish she dared not give in to. There weren't enough tears in the world to relieve that depth of sorrow.

A scant moment ago, they'd been utterly destitute and alone in the world. But things had changed. They were still ragged, to be sure, pale and gaunt from near starvation, and dirty from digging. And still alone. But no longer destitute.

As she watched Rahel cinch the mouth of the sack and tuck it securely inside her coat, a verse Corrie ten Boom had often quoted flooded Marie's mind. *My God shall supply all your need according to his riches in glory by Christ Jesus.* "But—are you sure you want to share your family's treasure with me?" she asked.

"Of course. Why should I need all of it, just one person? You are my very dearest—indeed, my only—friend in this world. I will give some to Josep and Ania for helping us. And you will take half of what remains. I insist. You will need it."

"Nie!" Marie exclaimed. "I cannot take so much."

Rahel regarded her evenly. "I have been thinking about this for a long time. When I realized we were going to survive Ravensbruck, the thought came to me. I shall go to Palestine, my people's homeland. I have never been there. I shall live in Jerusalem, our Holy City. Make jewelry, perhaps. Like Papa. He would like that."

Marie brushed straight blond bangs from her eyes and stared, awed by the dreamy expression subtracting lines of suffering, one by one, from Rahel's exquisite features. In their place, her classic beauty rose to the fore, despite the pallid complexion and dirt smudges, despite ill-fitting clothes and the dull, chopped hair peeking out from beneath her boyish hat.

"And what about me?" Marie asked, a sudden sense of awe surging through her as she tucked a few strands of lifeless hair back inside her cap.

"You, dearest friend, will go to America. The land of hope."

"Go to America!"

"Josep and Ania have contacts to help us reach the American sector. They say Jews are the only ones who have no trouble leaving Poland. Josep can obtain forged papers stating you are Jewish, get us both to Switzerland. From there we can go where we want." Smiling sweetly, she took out the sack and reached into it, withdrawing a Star of David on a fine gold chain. She slipped it over Marie's head, letting the medallion fall inside the shirt Marie had tucked into her baggy trousers. "There. This will help."

Still somewhat in awe, Marie fingered the necklace through her shirt. "But I don't know a soul in America."

"And who do you know here? Our families have been taken from us." Rahel stood and spun in a slow circle, her thin arms flung wide. "Look around. Where are the crowds that used to leave the city to bask in the quiet countryside? There is no one in sight. The only people we have seen are strangers. You must go where there is life. Make a new start."

The notion took on credibility as Marie Therese mulled it over. And gradually she understood the wisdom in her friend's words. She would go to America.

But a single thought sank into her heart, cruel and cold as the Ravensbruck barracks. A new life would be a thousand times lonelier.

In America she would not have Rahel. . .the only one who understood her special shame. Her curse.

one

New York City, Spring 1946

"What means this—*babe,* this *chick?*" Mary Theresa asked, moving to the dressing table for a closer look at herself. "Like infant I am? My legs, they are too skinny?" Turning sideways, she eyed her reflection in the pinkish light streaming through the bedroom's dotted swiss curtains.

Mr. and Mrs. Chudzik had fed her well in the six months she had been living in their home. Even she could see that her once emaciated frame had lost the bony contours. And her honey blond hair had grown considerably, recapturing much of its former length and shine. With her now Americanized name—from Marie Therese to Mary Theresa, her new, fashionable hairstyle, and a wardrobe with an abundance of long sleeves to conceal the evidence of her imprisonment, only her halting English set her apart from other young women her age.

She repositioned a bobby pin in the poufed roll of hair behind her ear as the mirrored images of Christine and Veronica Chudzik, the young daughters of the household, conquered the giggles brought on by her questions.

"No, Silly," dark-haired Veronica said, her heart-shaped face sobering. Two years older than her thirteen-year-old sibling, she always assumed the lead. "It is nothing. Babe and chick are *dobrze.* Good. It means the young men think you're pretty."

Mary frowned. Young men were the last thing on her mind and would likely remain so. "Much better to use proper English. *Nie rozumiem.* I not understand foolish American words."

15

"But you're learning," Christine reminded her, childish features alight with leftover remnants of mirth. "I think Mama is right. You learn faster if we only use Polish to explain things. It makes you have to start thinking in English."

Mary could only agree, though she'd considered the stringent household rule somewhat harsh at first.

"And," Veronica piped in, "you start your job next week. Soon you'll be out on your own and settled into your new apartment." She drew her knees to her chest and hugged them.

Christine brushed a flaxen braid over her shoulder, her smile wilting. "I'll miss you when you leave. It's been fun having you share our room."

This lovely room. Mary Theresa glanced around. So much fancier than hers had been in the Old Country. Rose-patterned wallpaper, cheerful rugs on the varnished floor. And so big for just two girls, she'd thought upon arriving. The spacious apartment in a multistoried brownstone building in Manhattan's Upper East Side had all but swallowed her up with its roominess. Her own tiny walk-up, more than a dozen blocks away and off Second Avenue, would be nowhere near so elegant. How had Rahel Dubinsky fared in Jerusalem?

Swallowing down loneliness for her dear Jewish friend, she crossed to the pair and put an arm about each of them. The sweet innocence that shone from their azure eyes was a sad reminder of a part of her own life that could never be undone. "And already I am missing you. Little sisters you are to me." Mustering all her effort, she feigned a cheery air, a wry smile tugging at her mouth. "Perhaps you teach me more foolish words, so I am knowing what these Americans say."

"Girls," their mother's voice called from the floor below, "I could use some help with supper."

"Yes, Mother," Veronica answered, getting up. She grinned at Mary. "We'll work on your English later."

The threesome hurried downstairs, the girls heading to the kitchen, and Mary Theresa to the linen closet for a fresh tablecloth. Mrs. Chudzik liked supper to be special, since it was the one meal when the whole family gathered together, first at the dining table, then afterward around the big radio in the parlor.

Mary had taken to the couple at once. Their plump short frames were the exact opposite of her own late parents', but both Mr. and Mrs. Chudzik were intelligent and loving and showed real concern for her. The family-like atmosphere reminded her of her own roots. And the fact that their children were both girls had been a bonus. Mary found it hard not to feel uncomfortable in the presence of men, young or old.

Tonight would be one of the last she'd be with these kind people who had helped many newcomers over the years to adjust to life in the new land. It was important that her transition to American life took place as smoothly as possible. So as they had done with others, they'd taken her into their home and their lives, made sure she attended Mass regularly, and treated her as a member of the family. She tried not to think about how much she would miss them all. Or how truly alone she would be living in a place by herself.

She felt as if she'd spent the last few years of her life saying good-bye to everyone she ever knew.

❧

Leaden clouds dragged across the city, enshrouding the tops of skyscrapers and coating their sides with drizzle, leaving a sheen on the streets below. The fine mist added streaks in the line of small, sooty glass panes high up on the Olympic Sewing Factory on 34th Street. Only the sickliest light penetrated the window grime even on the best of days, and on dull ones the windows were utterly worthless.

Inside the ancient building, a raft of black electrical cords dangled from the high ceiling like so many snakes, the exposed light bulbs casting a harsh, brassy glare across endless rows of women bent over their work. The incessant clacking of Singer sewing machines drowned out any hope of conversation—something which was not advisable during working hours, close confines or not. Everyone knew that too much visiting resulted in raised quotas.

Occupying one of the Singers, Mary Theresa grabbed a cutout shirtsleeve and partially finished cuff from the stacks at her side and positioned them for assembly before starting her treadle. As a newly hired, inexperienced employee, she'd been delegated to one of the older foot-powered models which interspersed the lot at random. The more proficient laborers used the much faster electric machines. Mary had worked steadily all morning, determined to reach her quota by day's end.

Most of all, she did not want to attract undue attention of the taskmistress, Mrs. Hardwick. With her large-boned, stocky frame, sharp nose, and short frizzy hair, the woman seemed a replica of one of the guards at Ravensbruck. She was only slightly more pleasant in the somber suit, plain white blouse, and black-laced shoes which made up her typical attire.

"Pssst."

Mary cut a glance at Estelle Thomas, at the electric machine to the right.

Her coworker did not slow her own work but tipped her head pointedly toward the floor.

A stack of finished sleeves had toppled off Mary Theresa's machine. She smiled her thanks to the friendly brunette and snatched them up, brushing the bottom one free of dust before eagle-eyed Mrs. Hardwick skulked by to find fault. The last thing she needed was for the woman to dock her pay or raise the quota to some unattainable number as punishment.

Mary found the job at the sewing factory tedious, but her limited English did not instill enough confidence in herself to seek something better. The long hours occupied a good part of her existence, and the wages, however meager, did provide her living expenses. Only a small sum of the money from Rahel remained in the savings account Mrs. Chudzik had opened for her—a balance she hoped to add to for night classes in English, typing, and shorthand someday. The greater part of the funds had paid for the necessary bribes and her fare to America, plus room and board to the Chudziks during the months she stayed in their home. It had also purchased new clothes and some necessities for her furnished apartment.

At last, the noon whistle shrilled. The rows of machines ceased operation, their cacophony immediately replaced by the drone of chatter and of chairs scooting back to form circles here and there among the tired-looking mass of women.

"Finally!" Estelle exclaimed, her thick-lashed sable eyes sparkling as she brushed a wisp of damp, curly hair from her temple. "I'm starving." She cleared her work space for room enough to eat, then reached into her bottom drawer and withdrew a lunch sack.

Mary did the same. "I, too, feel hungry."

The willowy young woman peered up at the windows, and a grimace replaced the ever-present smile on her rosy lips. "I hate it when the weather's too cool and miserable for us to go outside for a breath of fresh air." Removing the waxed paper from a sandwich, she set it out, releasing the unmistakable smell of tuna salad into the room's stuffy atmosphere while she poured hot tea from a thermos bottle.

"We stop the work for short time. That I am glad for."

Estelle nodded, her piquant face serene as she bowed her dark head for a quick prayer of thanks before taking a bite.

Somewhat uncomfortable at public displays of that nature, Mary waited respectfully until her new friend's prayer ended, then devoured her own cold cheese sandwich. It was a far cry from the sumptuous fare she'd enjoyed with the Chudziks, but the best she could throw together before dashing out the door to catch the trolley this morning.

"Think you'll make your quota this time?" Estelle asked, her feminine features accenting her sincerity.

Mary Theresa cocked her head. "I try. I keep trying till I do. Maybe today. Maybe soon."

"You're a good worker. I think you'll make it." A confident nod accompanied the statement.

"And if I do, it is because you help," Mary had to admit. "I know nothing when I first start here."

"Hey, we all had to start sometime, Mary. And I've enjoyed having such a conscientious worker next to me. The last girl was forever grousing about one thing or another. Never failed to put me in a bad mood—to say nothing of constantly aggravating Mrs. Hardwick." Rolling her eyes, she finished the last bite of her sandwich, then washed it down with some tea.

Gobbling her own food so quickly had done little to satisfy Mary's appetite. She tried not to notice the delicious-looking cookies her new friend was unwrapping, liberally speckled with chunks of chocolate and walnuts.

"Would you care for one?" Estelle asked, holding them out. "I don't think I can eat them both."

"If you are sure." More than grateful for the treat, Mary nodded her thanks.

"I am. In fact, I'll be baking more tonight—my brother's orders. Now that sugar rationing has ended, we've been enjoying some treats we've been missing." Her eyes widened. "Hey! Why not come home with me after work? I could use the help with baking, and you could have supper with us. I live only a couple of stops past yours. I'll see that you get on the right trolley afterward."

Mary stopped chewing. "I. . .think not. But thank you."

"Please, Mary?" Estelle urged. "I really like our working here together, and I've mentioned you so often to my family, they're dying to meet you. You do live alone, right?"

"Yes, but—"

"Then wouldn't you enjoy a good hot meal—with some other people as nice as me?"

The light tone and big grin assured Mary that the girl was teasing. But she wasn't altogether certain she should accept the offer, tempting or not. She opened her mouth to voice a polite refusal, but the bell to resume work cut her off.

"At least think about it," Estelle pressed as she swung around to her machine and turned it on. "Promise?"

"I will think about it."

In truth, it was all Mary Theresa thought about for the end-less hours which made up the remainder of the workday. She'd been out on her own for three weeks now, and though the Chudziks occasionally popped in to see how she was far-ing, it wasn't the same as living with them. No lively chatter enlivened her tiny kitchen table at mealtimes. In fact, their parting gift, a small table radio, only made Mary homesick for the laughter that would erupt among the family over a humorous comment by Jack Benny or George Burns and Gracie Allen. When the programs ended, even the most lively big-band music seemed a letdown.

She had started skipping Mass, also. The ornate beauty of the cathedral seemed impersonal, and once-beloved rituals no longer offered the kind of substance for which her heart yearned. She finally tucked her rosary and prayer book into one of her drawers, rarely taking them out. Mary still wore the Star of David Rahel had given her and had added a tiny crucifix to the chain. It seemed somehow symbolic of the friendship which had drawn them together.

But after years of being crammed into a too crowded bar-racks, plus several months sharing a room with two sweet, bubbly girls, the solitude she had once yearned for now seemed oppressive. She almost looked forward to coming to work, simply to hear other voices—and even more important, because of the growing friendship between her and Estelle. What could it hurt to accept that invitation, to liven up at least one lonely evening?

"Well, have you decided?" her coworker asked hopefully after the quitting time bell sounded and the muslin covers were being placed over the machines. "Please say yes."

Mary just smiled. Even if she had intended to refuse, Estelle's expression would have thwarted that plan. "I will come," she told her, and the two of them grabbed their umbrellas and handbags and filed out with the rest of the throng.

"Do I look all right?" Mary asked when they emerged into the dwindling light of day, where a playful gust of wind snatched long gold hairs from her neatly pinned roll and tossed them into her eyes. She tied on a triangular *babushka*. "I am dirty from factory."

"No worse than me," came Estelle's cheery response as she opened her umbrella. "You can freshen up at my house. Oh, I am so glad you're coming!" And with that, she linked an arm through Mary Theresa's, unmindful of such mundane matters as puddles or umbrella spokes that bumped together all the way to the trolley stop.

I hope I will be as glad, Mary thought. *Or will this just be more people I will grow to love. . .only to have to give them up?*

two

"That's it. I'm outa here." Jonathan Gray shoved his chair back from the card table by the parlor windows and unfolded his long legs to stand.

Nelson Thomas peered up from the checkerboard and smirked at his lanky best friend. "Isn't that a touch extreme? You've only lost six games. . .in a row."

The off-duty policeman didn't crack a smile. "Just isn't my day, Buddy. I gotta get to the precinct anyway. I drew the night shift this week." He plunked his uniform cap atop his sandy head and crossed the width of the room in three strides.

"Catch a lot of bank robbers," Nelson quipped, lacing his fingers behind his neck to stretch his shoulders.

"Will do. Gotta keep the streets safe for Mr. Average Citizen. See ya." With a mock salute, the cop shut the front door almost noiselessly behind himself.

While his pal clomped down the steps and away, Nelson returned his attention to the scattered red and black pieces. He scooped up the checkers and replaced them in their cardboard container, then folded the game board and stood it on end beside the bookcase. He debated about working some more on the picture puzzle he'd started before but decided against it.

At that moment, his mother bustled into the room, her slight form creating a breeze which stirred the graying permed hair framing her rosy cheeks. A frown etched twin lines above her button nose. "Jon left?" she asked, drying her hands on a dish towel. "I was going to invite him for supper."

"He was in a hurry, Mom. Had to go to work."

"Oh, and just when I made too much. Well, I suppose we can eat leftovers tomorrow." Draping the damp towel over the shoulder of the bib apron covering her housedress, she gathered the empty iced tea glasses the two men had drained, then headed back up the hall toward the kitchen.

Watching after her until she left his range of vision, Nelson marveled over her inherent need to mother all the young people who darkened their doors. Especially the ones like his pal, who had no moms of their own. Stray young people, stray puppies and kittens, they were all the same to her. Dad had picked a real gem for himself.

Thought I had, too. Once. Immediately shirking off that painful reminder, Nelson used his crutch as leverage to ease himself to a standing position and hobbled to the overstuffed easy chair he preferred, ignoring the vinyl-covered hassock as he sank onto the seat cushion. He switched on the radio, turning the dial in search of some lively Benny Goodman or other upbeat tunes. Anything to keep his mind too occupied to dwell on that loss. . .or the other one.

The front door opened, admitting his sister, Estelle, on a round of giggles that made her sound twelve years old instead of just two years younger than his own twenty-three. She and a honey blond Nelson had never seen before stuck closed umbrellas into a stand just inside, then looped their shoulder bags and kerchiefs over the hall tree.

Presuming the pair would head upstairs to Stella's room, Nelson relaxed against the comfortable chair back and focused again on Glenn Miller's rendition of "Little Brown Jug."

But they didn't leave. He cringed as his sister's footsteps headed his way, hers and the other girl's. And Stella knew he wasn't at ease around strangers—hadn't been since he'd come home from the war. Later, he'd drive that point home to her one more time, make her understand. After all, a guy deserved some privacy.

"Nel-se," she sing-songed, making two syllables out of one as she came up beside him, "I've brought my friend from work home with me. She's going to help me bake cookies after supper."

"That's swell, Sis," he said, not bothering to camouflage his facetious tone.

"I'd like you to meet Mary Theresa Malinowski," she went on. "You've heard me mention her before. Mary, this is my brother, Nelson. He likes to boss his baby sister around, but I don't let him get to me."

Reluctantly, he slid his gaze up to meet the visitor's.

Nelson stared into a face as gorgeous and perfectly rendered as any porcelain doll's. And the largest, most beautiful eyes he had ever seen mesmerized him. A luminous, celestial blue-green, and fringed by long, silky lashes, they were filled with what appeared to be outright. . .*fear*. She looked twice as uncomfortable as he, if such a thing were possible. He offered a reserved smile. "Glad to meet you, Mary."

"I, too, am pleased," she whispered with an almost imperceptible nod, her creamy skin every bit as white as the blouse she wore with her plaid skirt. But the way she shrank a fraction backward added the anticipated dash of doubt to the polite words issued by those rose-petal lips.

It didn't appear as if Estelle noticed anything unusual, however. "Well, come on, Mare. I'll introduce you to Mom. It's still a little early for my dad to come home from our butcher shop, but he's always in time for supper."

As they walked away, Nelson beheld Mary's cameo-like profile in awe.

࿇

Mary Theresa struggled to gather her composure. A father she could deal with. But had Estelle mentioned a grown brother at home? If she had, that little detail had gotten lost in the noise of sewing machines being started up again after the noon break. If she'd caught it, she never would have agreed to come here.

But turning away from Nelson Thomas in the upholstered chair, her gaze had landed on something she had not noticed before—the turned-up trouser leg. He was missing his left limb from just below the knee. Her heart contracted. Except for some grim lines alongside his mouth and a slight downward turn of his light brown eyes, Estelle's lean, mahogany-haired brother had an amiable enough face. Even handsome, in a timeless sort of way—if she were the least bit interested—which of course she was not. Reinforced by a determination to ignore that square jaw and those finely honed features, she steeled herself against what nevertheless might turn out to be a very long evening and tagged after her friend.

The Chudziks' apartment had been quite lovely, furnished in fine woods and rich textiles. But this tenement house, Mary decided on the way through the hall, emitted a nearly tangible quality of homeyness that the more elegant residence had lacked. Even though the floral runner showed definite worn paths, and the drapes and slipcovers looked faded and threadbare in spots, the whole place seemed to welcome her and make her feel at ease.

The delicious aroma of beef stew grew stronger as they neared the kitchen and entered. This room also exuded a decidedly cheery atmosphere, whether from the red and white decor and crisp gingham curtains or the roomy expanse of work space, she couldn't be sure. At least, not until Estelle approached the stove and tapped the shoulder of the petite-framed woman standing in front of it.

"Mom?"

She paused from stirring the pot of stew and turned around, the smile on her face looking as if it had been born there and never left.

"Yes, Dear."

"I brought company for supper. This is Mary. Mary Theresa Malinowski. We work together at Olympic. I've told you about her."

The smile broadened, adding an engaging light to small hazel eyes as she reached out to lay a hand on Mary's forearm. "Yes. How lovely to meet you, Mary. I'm so glad you've come."

"Mrs. Thomas," she answered, noting the sincerity in the woman's expression and manner. It differed very little from Estelle's, she realized, appreciating the strong resemblance. No wonder her daughter had seemed so pleasant and helpful to a brand-new employee, growing up with such a mother.

"Can we do anything to help?" her friend asked. "Set the table? Make lemonade?"

"Not a thing. It's all done. You two just run along and have a nice visit. We'll eat as soon as your father comes in from work."

"Well, come upstairs then, Mary," Estelle suggested. "We can freshen up before supper."

Mary snagged her handbag from the hall tree on their way to the staircase and accompanied the young woman to her room.

They'd barely finished sponging their faces and running a comb through their hair when the summons came, and the two of them hurried down to the dining room, where the rest of the family had already gathered around the oblong maple table. Mary admired the embroidered red roses on the tablecloth as she and Estelle each claimed one of the two remaining places.

Not without a twinge of uneasiness did Mary notice her chair was directly across from her friend's brother. And gracing the wall behind him she spied a beautifully framed portrait of Christ, without the sacred heart she was accustomed to seeing.

The old nuns at school would be shocked, she thought with chagrin. Not only had their prize student consorted with Jews, but now was being entertained by Protestants!

"Ah. Stella has brought a guest, I see." Light from the fixture overhead glinted on the receding hairline and bifocals belonging to the congenial-looking man who occupied the head of the table as he glanced from Mary to his daughter. His wiry, muscular build and strong hands gave evidence of hard work.

"Oh, I almost forgot," she said lightly. "Dad, this is Mary Theresa Malinowski, my friend from work. I imposed on her good nature to help me make cookies after supper."

"I see. Well, how do you do, Mary? We're glad you could join us."

"Mr. Thomas," she said politely, noting that the man seemed every bit as gracious as his wife, and he possessed an open, honest face that put her at ease.

"Now that everyone's present and accounted for, we'll return thanks," he said with a jovial smile. He bowed his head, and everyone followed suit.

"Dear Lord, thank You for Your wonderful provision day by day and for the opportunity to share our bounty with friends. Please bless this food and our conversation around the table. And thank You for bringing Mary to our home. May this be the first of many happy visits. We ask You to grant her a special blessing this evening and in the days to come. In Jesus' name, amen.

"Amen," the others echoed, and Mary crossed herself.

Having used recited prayers for so many occasions in her life, the intimate tone of Mr. Thomas's prayer brought Mary's prison mate, Corrie ten Boom, to her mind. As the older man began ladling rich stew from the china tureen into bowls and passing them around, she marveled at the way some people seemed able to approach Almighty God in such a casual, friendlike fashion.

"Would you care for bread?"

Estelle's voice coaxed Mary back from her musings. . .as did the realization that Nelson was staring at her. "Oh. Yes, thank you," she mumbled, lowering her lashes. She accepted the heaping plate and removed a slice before passing it to Mrs. Thomas on her left.

"So, Mary," the man of the house began, "tell us about yourself. Have you and your family been in New York long?"

She didn't relish becoming the center of attention, much less receiving personal questions that might lead to her shameful past. But after filling her spoon with succulent beef broth to cool, she met his gaze. "My family is no more. From Poland I come to stay with American family. With the English language they help me till a job I could get."

"Oh, you poor dear," Estelle's mother murmured, administering a loving pat to Mary's arm, her expression revealing a tender heart.

Her husband blanched. "I didn't mean to pry. Forgive me."

Mary feigned a tight smile to no one in particular. "It is. . . how you say. . .okay."

"Mary works on the machine next to mine," Estelle piped up. "She's only been with Olympic for a couple weeks and should be making her quota any day now. She lets me talk my head off whenever I want—when we're allowed to visit, of course. Usually the noon break."

"But do you keep her supplied with aspirin?" Nelson muttered with a subtle curl of his lip. "For the headaches."

"No headaches," Mary responded. "I am liking her talk."

He smirked. "Just wait till the novelty wears off."

"Novelty?" Mary had to ask. "This I not understand."

"Don't pay any attention to that brother of mine," Estelle said, rolling her eyes. "It's best to ignore him."

But Mary Theresa caught the mischievous twitch of Nelson's mouth, and the sight resurrected the long ago days when her own brothers would tease her mercilessly. And somehow, she didn't mind the bittersweet memory, even if the present banter did happen to be at her expense. She returned her attention to the hearty stew before her as the father of the house began regaling everyone with amusing stories about some of his butcher shop's regular customers and how glad everyone was to see the end of meat rationing.

After they'd finished the stew and generous slices of fresh apple pie, Mr. Thomas reached behind him for a small leather-bound book on the lace-doilied buffet and read aloud a collection of Scripture verses pertaining to hope.

Once more, Mary was transported back in time to Ravensbruck. She could hear in her mind the surprisingly strong voice of the older woman from Holland, hear again some of the very same wondrous promises that had remained in her memory to this day. It seemed a fitting end to supper, one she would ponder later in her solitude. But now, however, as Estelle stood and began clearing the table, she knew it was on to dishes and baking.

Hours later than normal, Mary Theresa finally got back to her apartment. She still smelled of cookie dough, could still taste the satin sweetness of the chipped chocolate, melted and warm from the oven. After hooking the handle of her umbrella over the doorknob, she switched the floor lamp on, then draped her raincoat over the camelback sofa which dominated her combination dining/sitting room. As she kicked off her loafers, her gaze surveyed her surroundings.

Compared to some of the other residences she had seen in America, her diminutive abode seemed stark and uninviting. The Chudziks had seen to it that she had curtains and linens and other basic necessities. But the walls lacked adornment. The whole place needed some bright, homey touches. Perhaps some weekend she'd prevail upon Estelle to come shopping with her. The girl had made no mention of a regular boyfriend, and she might know where to find some good bargains, assuming she wasn't always busy with her family.

Her family. Mary's heart swelled at the remembrance of the kind people who made up Estelle's world, the way they had taken her in. She couldn't help smiling. Mrs. Thomas had fluttered about the kitchen like a mother hen, yet never really intruded, while her daughter and Mary baked a double batch of cookies. Her husband, who had not repeated his blunder of probing for personal information at the table, had retired to the parlor after supper to read the evening paper.

But Nelson. Mary's smile took a pensive turn when thoughts surfaced of her friend's brooding older brother with the perceptive brown eyes. Despite definite laugh lines alongside his mouth, smiles had been few. He hadn't exactly been friendly, but neither had he been unfriendly.

In truth, Mary didn't quite know what to make of him. And perhaps that was just as well.

three

Mary brushed lingering bread crumbs from her polka-dot dress, then took another drink of the hot tea she'd brought for lunch.

"Looks like you're doing great today," Estelle commented between bites of her sandwich as she eyed Mary's stack of finished sleeves.

"Yes. My quota I should make, I think, this time."

"I wouldn't be surprised." Her friend paused. "My parents sure enjoyed meeting you last night. I hardly ever take someone home with me. They really like you." She offered her two cookies from the batch they'd baked.

"Thank you." Mary lifted one of them to her nose and inhaled deeply. "So much better it smells than this place."

"I agree. Completely."

"I am liking your family, too. So friendly they are." Munching the treat, she mentally replayed the visit.

"Even Nelson thought you seemed. . .let's see, how did he put it? Oh, yeah. Decent. He thought you were pretty decent."

Mary swallowed a little too quickly, but recovered. "What means 'decent'?" She suspected she already knew the definition, but some American words had a variety of meanings. In this particular instance, she needed specifics.

"Oh, you know. Swell. Nice. It's about as much of a compliment as he gives these days, grump that he is."

Estelle's response unraveled the tightness around Mary's spirit.

"He's been in a black mood ever since he came home from the rehabilitation center," she went on. "Thinks his life is over. He hardly does anything except sit around and mope. He never used to be like that."

"Wounded at war your brother is?"

Estelle nodded. "In France. He almost didn't make it, really. He was in the hospital for quite a long time, before—" The end-of-lunch bell overpowered the last part of the sentence.

Pursing her lips, Mary Theresa wrapped the remaining cookie and tucked it inside her handbag, then moved her chair into place to resume working.

She didn't want to think about Nelson Thomas. At all. He was too attractive. And too—his own word fit perfectly— decent. Too decent for someone like her. No man would ever want her now. She'd accepted that cruel reality long ago. But still, the teasing remarks he'd made to his sister and the quirk of his mouth when he had chided Estelle made Mary miss her own siblings, particularly Aleksandr and Patryk, the two who had been closest to her own age. How unfair it was that such handsome, strong youths had been put to death merely to satisfy the whim of a Nazi lunatic who hadn't known either one of them—or any others among the countless millions who had been exterminated. She only hoped her brothers had not been first made to suffer.

"Pssst."

A quick look at her coworker, and Mary caught the warning in her eyes. Mrs. Hardwick was marching purposely toward them. Plucking a set of sleeve parts from her work piles, Mary immediately positioned them under the presser foot on the machine and started pumping the treadle. She felt the keen stare boring into her back when the woman paused momentarily behind her before slowly moving on.

Halfway through the afternoon, while Estelle left her machine to replenish her supply of shirt sections, Mary went to use the facilities. It drew a stern glower from the supervisor but couldn't be helped. In the briefest of moments, she was back at her station and working steadily until the end of the shift.

This had been her best day yet. She'd kept a running tally of each dozen she added to her basket and knew she'd done it—finally reached the magical number which at first had seemed an impossible goal. With a triumphant grin at Estelle, she stood to collect the completed sleeves to be turned in and logged next to her name in the ledger.

She felt the blood drain from her face as she stared at the pathetic pile.

In the middle of covering her electric machine, Estelle stopped. "What's wrong?"

"Gone!" Mary croaked through her clenched throat. "Almost half of my sleeves. Gone."

Her coworker leaned to peer into Mary's basket, her expression registering shock. "It can't be. I watched your work accumulating all through the day. I know you had to have made your quota."

The heavy footsteps of the supervisor grew louder on her approach. "Got a problem here, Malinowski?"

Mary's insides turned over at Mrs. Hardwick's insinuating look.

"I–I—"

"Someone helped herself to Mary Theresa's finished pile," Estelle answered for her.

"Is that right? And who might that be?" the woman challenged, cold gray eyes darting from her to Mary and back. "The girl hasn't made her quota once in all the time she's been here."

"She would have today," Estelle insisted.

Mrs. Hardwick tapped the toe of one black shoe impatiently and tucked her chin. "Well, we don't really know that, now, do we?"

"I. . .am sorry," Mary somehow managed. "Harder I will work tomorrow."

"You're right about that, little lady," she answered, each word precise and flat. "Your quota will rise by two dozen, beginning tomorrow morning. I suggest you get here early and spend more time at your machine and less at the lavatory."

Two dozen more! Mary swallowed her rising panic and stood tall. "Yes, Madam."

"And if you aren't turning in your daily requirements by the end of this week, there are plenty of other applicants waiting for work. Remember that." Without further comment, the supervisor turned and hiked away.

Once Mrs. Hardwick was out of earshot, Estelle hugged Mary. "I am so sorry. I can't figure out how such a thing could have happened."

"It is. . .all right," she whispered. "This quota I make. I make the new one."

Subdued, they gathered their belongings and left to catch the trolley, neither of them making their usual small talk along the way. But once they were seated and on the homeward journey, Estelle shook her head. "I don't know how you could be so gracious to that old witch."

Mary shrugged, recalling more of fellow prisoner Corrie ten Boom's admonitions at the death camp. "A job she has, like us. To turn in much work done each day. What is expected I will do."

Estelle regarded her evenly. "You sound like our pastor. 'Turn the other cheek.' I used to think I could do that without any effort at all. But not today. My temper's always been my worst fault. And this afternoon it would have given me great pleasure to punch her in the face."

"A good teacher I had," Mary admitted. "And wise. So wise." She averted her attention to the passing buildings, especially enjoying the little groups of children at play on the side streets. So healthy and carefree they looked, as children should.

A few silent moments lapsed.

"Doing anything for supper tonight?" Estelle asked, a ray of hope gleaming in her face.

Mary had to smile. "Yes. A hot bath I am taking. Then a bowl of soup. Chicken noodle."

"My favorite."

"Sometime soon I make two cans. For you to eat with me."

"I would like that. Truly. But everybody should have some real home cooking now and then. Ever had pasties?"

Confusion clouded Mary's mind. "The word I not know."

"They're delicious," Estelle answered. "Kind of a meat and potato pie, served with broth or gravy over top. My mom makes the absolute best ones in the world. I'll invite you over next time we're having some."

"Already it is making me hungry," Mary teased. Standing to pull the cord, she gave her friend's shoulder an affable squeeze. "My stop, this is. See you tomorrow."

"Bright and early," Estelle teased. "Don't forget."

🙟

"We're off to prayer meeting, Son," Nelson heard his father say on his way into the parlor. He wore his customary suit and tie, his Bible under one arm. "Sure you won't come with us?"

Nelson returned his gaze to the open book he'd been trying to concentrate on, but without success. He shook his head.

"Maybe next time, then," his mother suggested, tugging on white cotton gloves that complemented her church hat as she joined them. "The pastor's been presenting a wonderful study on 'The Cross through the Scriptures.' We're enjoying it immensely."

"That's good, Mom. I'll see you both when you get home." He buried his nose a fraction deeper, to miss seeing that pained look on her face. His parents meant well, he knew. But what they didn't seem to acknowledge was that he could no longer dredge up much enthusiasm for churchgoing—

even though Pastor Herman had once been one of his biggest heroes. Sure, church had been pretty important before he went off to join the army, but that was then. A lot of water had gone under the bridge since those days. A lot.

He made another attempt to read the same page, then gave up and closed the book.

Barely ten minutes elapsed before Stella breezed in. "Oh, no. I missed Mom and Dad, huh?"

"You got it."

"Rats." Without removing her cardigan or hanging her shoulder bag, she plopped on the couch adjacent to his chair, letting her head fall back in defeat, her hands crossed atop her abdomen. "I got held up past quitting time at work. And I really need more practice on that new choir number for Sunday, too."

Nelson cocked a brow. "So what do you want from me, a piggyback ride?"

Straightening, Estelle leveled a glare on him, one that gained heat by the second. "If you must know, I don't want anything from you," she snapped. "You've been nothing but a pain since you came home, and I've about had it up to here with that poor-me attitude of yours." With a huff, she rose to her feet.

He opened his mouth to respond, but she didn't give him a chance.

"I had a bad day at work—or at least Mary did—and now I'm missing church because of it. So I'd appreciate it if you'd just—just—"

"Wait a minute, Sis," he cut in calmly, raising a palm like a traffic cop. "What happened at work? Why don't you calm down and tell big brother your troubles. It'll make you feel better."

Her expression gradually softened, turning to a blush with her sheepish smile. "Sorry for blowing up, Nelse. I didn't mean what I said. I promise."

He gave an offhanded shrug. "I know. But I probably deserve it. Everybody else is walkin' on eggshells around me. At least you level with me, get honest once in awhile."

"Honest, maybe, but hardly tactful."

"Hey, that's what sisters are for, right? But for now, the subject is you, not me. So what happened at work?"

Estelle moistened her lips. "It concerns Mary, really. She's been trying hard to make her production quota—"

"And?" he probed, impatient, yet not knowing why.

"Well, the thing is, she finally did it this afternoon. She was so proud."

"So? What'd they do, throw the girl a party? Is that why you're late? I thought you said this was a bad day."

"This would be a little easier if you'd quit cutting in," she reminded him.

With a repentant grin, he gestured for her to take the floor once more.

"Anyway," she continued, "I watched her working all day long, saw the pile growing higher and higher in her basket. I know she made her quota, if not better than that. . .only, when she went to turn it in, someone had snitched a good half of it, if not more."

Nelson raised both eyebrows this time, but did not say anything.

"Mary was absolutely white with shock. Old Lady Hardwick was her usual magnanimous self, full of tea and sympathy. Ha! Insults and insinuations were all that came out of that mean mouth. She upped Mary's requirements two extra dozen. And she has to do it by Friday or she's out of a job. That's only two days from now."

"The woman's all heart. Sounds like my old drill sergeant back at boot camp."

Estelle almost laughed but turned serious again. "But you

know what surprised me the most? Mary. She just squared those shoulders of hers and said she'd work harder. She'd made this quota, and she'd do that one, too. It's the strangest thing. I was mad enough to spit nails at whoever took advantage of such a sweet-spirited girl. And there she is, telling me Mrs. Hardwick has a boss, too, and depends on the rest of us to keep her level of production high."

"You don't say." Nelson rubbed his jaw with a thumb and forefinger, trying to envision that wisp of a gal holding her own before the hard-nosed supervisor of Olympic Sewing Factory. No wonder Stella had been so upset with him for being such a smart alec.

Again he felt there was something indefinable about that Polish beauty. Mary seemed on a higher plane than most of the other girls he'd known. And her eyes. . .they had a haunting quality that caught at a person's heart. Coming from Poland, she had to have known a fair amount of suffering—especially if the rest of her family no longer existed. In all likelihood, her loved ones had met their ends at the hand of some beast of a Nazi.

And he'd lost only a leg.

Maybe a guy could afford to take a few lessons from Mary Theresa Malinowski.

four

Curled up on her couch in a flannel robe, her hair wrapped in a towel, Mary smiled at the banter between Jack Benny and his man, Rochester, issuing through the radio speaker. Even when she couldn't quite understand the jokes, she tried to enter into the spirit of the audience's laughter. After all, the more exposure to English, the better. She figured eventually she'd catch on to American humor. She kept the radio on most of the time she was home to help banish the awful stillness of the apartment, a quiet so deep she doubted she'd ever get used to it.

During the musical interlude between the end of the program and the beginning of the next, her thoughts drifted backward to the day's events at the factory. Someone else, among the throng of women who toiled long hours at Olympic, must have had a desperate need to reach a quota. But in dredging up the sea of faces which were still only vaguely familiar, Mary couldn't imagine who might have stolen her work.

In the death camp, poor performance resulted in a short walk to the ovens. . .an incentive for putting forth one's best efforts. But here at the factory the task of attaching cuffs to sleeves had finally become automatic for Mary. She had not the slightest doubt she'd be able to produce enough to keep Mrs. Hardwick satisfied.

It had been thoughtful of Estelle to stand up for her, though, and then, later, to suggest she come to another family meal. Listening to her friend's father reading Scripture after supper made her realize how much she missed the nightly readings she'd grown to rely on in the Ravensbruck barracks. She'd spied a Bible on the night table in Estelle's room and another on a bookshelf in the parlor. Perhaps on her next visit she might actually touch one, even open it. Let her eyes feast on the written words that had given her strength to survive.

Footsteps outside, followed by a knock on the door, startled her out of her reverie.

Mary got up and turned off the radio. Clutching the throat of her robe, she padded to answer the summons. "Who is outside?" she asked before turning the latch.

"It's me, Veronica."

"And Christine," a second voice supplied.

With no little relief, Mary let them both in, then glanced around for the girls' parents.

"It's just us," Veronica told her. "Mother and Father wanted to visit a sick friend from our parish, and we convinced them to drop us off on the way."

"We hope you don't mind," her sister added. "They said they wouldn't be too long."

"Mind!" Mary grabbed their petite forms in a huge hug. "Being alone I mind much more. Please, sit down. I change quick." She dashed to the bathroom, where tomorrow's skirt and blouse hung in readiness for the morning. Seconds later, she emerged dressed, with her damp hair fastened in a barrette at the nape of her neck.

"We stopped at the corner for some ice cream," Veronica said, holding out a small brown bag. "Chocolate, just for you."

"How well you know me, my little sisters. Oh, so glad to see you I am." Accepting the treat from the older girl, Mary stepped to the tiny kitchenette off the main room. She set the pint onto the sink's drain board and made short work of dipping the contents into three dishes.

"How is your new job?" Christine asked, delving into hers

the minute she was served.

"Fine. It is fine. Sleeves I make. For men's shirts."

Veronica turned up her pert nose. "Sounds boring."

"A living it is," Mary responded quietly. "To learn to sew is good." She took a leisurely spoonful of ice cream and studied the dear little faces she so sorely missed. Veronica's rich brown hair was as shiny as ever, parted in the middle with bangs. And Christine's braids sported bows that matched her navy jumper. In many ways, the tiny blond resembled Mary's dead sister, Janecska, which she found strangely comforting. "Everyone is well at your house?" she asked the younger girl.

She nodded. "Only it seems like someone is missing, without you."

"Have you made any friends, Mary?" Veronica placed the spoon in her empty dish, then set it on one of the lamp tables bracketing the sofa.

"Yes. One."

"A handsome man?" she teased, grinning.

For a split second, the face of Nelson Thomas taunted Mary's consciousness. She opened her mouth to offer a negative reply, but Christine spoke first.

"Mother told us not to be nosy," she rebuked Veronica, then turned to Mary. "Sissy only thinks about boys 'cause she's got a new boyfriend."

Her sibling gazed up to the ceiling. "Jason's *not* my boyfriend. Besides, he has too many freckles."

"My friend is from work," Mary blurted in an effort to restore the peace. "Estelle is her name. To her house I went last night for visit. We make cookies."

"I hope she's nice," Christine mused.

Mary nodded. "Very nice family she has. Friendly."

"Any brothers?" Veronica asked, that impish sparkle back again.

"Not of your age," she said with a wry grimace.

Christine made a face at her sister, then turned. "What's it like to work in a factory, anyway?"

For the next few minutes, she entertained the young pair with the lighter aspects of being new on a job, relishing the carefree sound of their girlish giggles.

But all too soon another knock signified the end of the visit, and Mrs. Chudzik came to collect her daughters.

"Some tea you would like?" Mary asked after returning the plump little woman's warm embrace.

"No, thank you, Dear. The girls need to get to bed for school. Perhaps another time. Everything okay with you?"

"Fine, yes."

A round of kisses and hugs and good-byes, and the lively bunch took their leave.

Mary held onto the knob as she watched the threesome head for the car parked out front. She mustered her brightest smile and waved down at Mr. Chudzik, then closed the door once again, not wanting to see them drive off.

Not wanting to hear it either, she hurried to the radio and turned it on, sighing when "Little Brown Jug" brought yet another reminder of Estelle's brother.

ॐ

Ho ho ho, you and me. Little brown jug, how I love thee. Nelson whistled under his breath to the accompaniment of the Glenn Miller tune as he shucked his shirt and trousers and slipped between the cool sheets, his crutches on the floor beside his bed. Not in the mood for a recanting of how wonderful the church service had been or how he should have been there, he had purposely retired to his room before his parents came home. Even with his bedside radio playing, they were considerate enough not to disturb him, which suited him just fine. He doused the light.

Cupping the back of his head, he gazed up at the darkened ceiling. He'd barely been out of this house in the three months since he'd been home. His friend Jon had been trying to persuade him to go out with him to a movie or a baseball game, and his mom and dad were forever after him to start going to Sunday and Wednesday services again. But Nelson couldn't abide other people's stares, the looks of pity—or worse, eyes averted altogether. He had plenty to occupy himself right here. Books, board games, daily crossword puzzles, radio programs. One of these days he might even tune in to *Stella Dallas* or *Pepper Young's Family*. . .see what Mom thought was so wonderful about soap operas.

A grim smile tweaked one side of his mouth. Some exciting life. And a far cry from the career in engineering which once had been his dream. He rarely allowed himself to indulge in poignant recollections of the bustling office where he'd apprenticed before going into the army. He could still picture that place, cluttered with rolls and stacks of blueprints, drawers filled with stubby drawing pencils and slide rules, hard hats perched atop file cabinets. That life was for the able-bodied, not someone who was half a man.

Even as he lay there, he felt a nagging tingle in his missing foot, as if nobody had informed his brain the shattered limb had been left behind in some field hospital across the ocean. The doctors at rehab alleged that those phantom itches would eventually subside. Nelson hoped it was true. He rolled onto his side and punched his pillow to a more comfortable shape.

Was Stella right? Had he sat around with a chip on his shoulder since coming back from the war? If so, it was a wonder his family could put up with him. He'd make a better effort at being cheerful from now on. Be more like. . .Mary.

Nelson made no attempt to banish visions of the fair, golden-haired beauty that drifted across his mind's eye. His family loved him and naturally sympathized with him over the wounds he'd suffered on the battlefields of France. But Mary Theresa was probably the only one who could really understand the depth of his loss. That conviction caused a peculiar expectancy in his stomach, an eagerness which pressed up against the underside of his heart.

Maybe she also needed someone to talk to. . . .

≈

"Hey, Mare, you can stop now," Estelle quipped a whole minute after the noon bell.

Mary nodded. Her shoulders sagged, and she ceased pumping the treadle. "This sleeve I wanted to finish. That is all."

Estelle eyed the growing stack in Mary's basket, then scrunched up her face. "You work any faster, and you'll even beat me!" She lowered her voice to a conspiratorial whisper. "Then the old bat will raise everybody's quota! Honestly," she added with a mischievous smirk, "the woman's stocking seams are so straight, her garters must hang from her shoulder blades."

Unable to stop a self-conscious grin as she unwrapped her sandwich, Mary met her friend's gaze. "To make only my quota I want today—plus one more. I do it; you will see." She bit off a corner of the bread.

"I believe you will. I've been watching you hunched over that old machine all morning without even stopping for a breath. Where in the world did you get such determination?"

If you only knew, Mary thought. "Hard teachers I had."

"I had no idea Polish schools were so strict."

"Not Polish," Mary corrected. "In Germany, the hard teachers." At the confusion clouding her friend's face, she sought a change of subject while she filled her thermos cup with steaming tea. "Some company I have last night. My American little sisters."

"Oh," Estelle breathed. "Your host family. How nice."

"Yes. To see them is good, Veronica and Christine. They bring ice cream. Chocolate, my favorite."

Her coworker smiled. "It's very considerate of those people

to keep track of you, make sure you're doing okay. Speaking of favorites, Mom says she'll make some pasties next week. Tuesday, perhaps. Will you come for supper?"

"I will come." The words popped out of their own accord, before Mary could muster a refusal.

The rest of the afternoon passed so swiftly, she remembered only a blur of white fabric passing from her left to the work-basket on her right. The quitting bell caught her by surprise. But she knew she'd made her goal—that, along with not just one, but two extras. With no little satisfaction, she clipped the threads on the final sleeve and added it to the others. Then she stood, easing the kink in her back.

"Good going, Mare!" Estelle murmured at her side. "Wait'l Hardwick checks your total today."

Mary picked up her work and straightened her shoulders, smiling all the way to the production counter.

Later that night, in her bed, she tried not to dwell too much on next week's meal with Estelle's family. She dared not let herself become attached to people. It only hurt later, when they were no longer around. She would simply enjoy each day as it came. Be thankful for the present, as Corrie ten Boom would have said.

And, her conscience admonished, no doubt Corrie would do whatever she could to encourage a soul who still suffered from the cruelties of war. . .like Nelson Thomas.

Even if he did happen to be a man.

The realization lingered on the edges of her heart.

five

Despite her misgivings about becoming too attached to Estelle's family, Mary couldn't help counting the days until Tuesday arrived. Home-cooked meals were a real treat in light of her limited cooking ability, and she was curious to see whether Mrs. Thomas's meat-and-potato pies were as tasty as her friend alleged.

She selected an emerald jumper from her wardrobe, plus a complementing print blouse with dark green piping around the collar and sleeves. The ensemble would look fairly presentable by the end of the day—at least, so she hoped. There was no reason she needed to dress up, she told herself, but a guest in someone's home should at least look neat.

Her skill and performance at the factory had continued to improve since she made her quota, which increased her confidence. But it was the friendship with Estelle that made her look forward to each weekday, especially this one. She relished even the smallest chance to spend time with her wavy-haired coworker. Lunchtimes seemed far too short in comparison to the hours when the noisy atmosphere precluded any real communication.

Humming as she uncovered her Singer, she smiled at Estelle and stowed her lunch bag and purse in the machine's bottom drawer.

"Ready for a bright new day?" Estelle asked cheerily, sweeping a glance around the dreary facility already filling with employees.

Mary's gaze followed the same course. "A place to work, it is."

"I can think of lots of places where I'd rather spend my time."

"Perhaps." A spark of mischief brought a saucy grin. "But me you would not have." The quip surprised even Mary. When had she last felt the lightness of spirit which made her want to joke with someone?

Estelle bubbled into a giggle. "Now I know why I like you. When you're around, a person doesn't *need* sunshine."

The trill of the starting bell prevented Mary from having to concoct a response. With a playful nod, she took her seat and focused on her production goal, hoping that this day, too, would pass quickly.

&

Unaccountably restless, Nelson leaned on his crutches and idly plunked a few notes on the upright piano which dominated a length of parlor wall, then gave up and made his way to the front window.

The usual after-school baseball game occupied the neighborhood boys out on the street, while a bit farther down the block, young girls chanted rhymes in the measured cadence of double Dutch, happy sounds which carried through the screens. Both sights made him feel old. It didn't seem so long ago that he and Jon would have been among those boisterous boys, and Stella would have been out there taking turns jumping rope or manning the ends for others. Where had those simple years gone?

"Such a nice day," his mother commented, coming to join him. "I always look forward to the warm days of summer."

"You like humidity, huh?" he wisecracked, still watching the kids at play.

"No, not humidity. The flowers, the fresh garden vegetables. I like knowing I'll soon be canning again, putting up a supply for winter when the cold days come and we're snowed in."

Nelson had to smile. Hectic canning days were among his most vivid memories of childhood. . .Mom and Stella, dwarfed by assorted piles of garden produce, their hair damp and frazzled and forming tiny ringlets around their faces as they worked. He could still conjure up the familiar smells of scalded, peeled tomatoes and peaches, the cinnamony scent of apples being cooked down to make endless quarts of sauce. And what a bounty for the pantry and cellar shelves! On the cold, rainy battlefields of Europe, he'd have given almost anything to find such delectable fare in his mess kit, instead of cold, monotonous K rations.

"Yeah, I know what you mean," he finally answered.

She slid an arm about his waist. "Can I get you anything? Fresh coffee? Tea? Lemonade?"

"Now that you mention it, I guess I am kind of thirsty. Thanks, Mom."

"Stella should be off work by now. She's bringing Mary Malinowski home with her for supper. My heart goes out to that little gal." She sighed. "All alone in the world, trying to adapt to life in a whole new country. So much pain in those young eyes, yet never a complaint. Even to Stella."

Had it been anyone else, Nelson would have taken the comment about not complaining as a personal affront. But he knew his mom, and knew her words came from deep inside. And he, too, sensed the war had taken an immeasurable toll on the young Polish woman. He'd caught the haunted longing in those eyes several times himself, when Mary wasn't aware of it.

"Makes a body want to say some extra prayers," his mom added on a wistful note, returning to the kitchen.

Until then, Nelson had been trying hard not to think about Mary Theresa. He'd convinced himself no woman could possibly be as naturally beautiful as she'd seemed on her first visit. And it might not be wise to get involved in problems he probably couldn't help her with, either. He took a seat in the easy chair, and in moments his mother brought him a tall glass of lemonade. "Thanks again."

She gave his arm a loving pat. "I do hope the girls come soon. I need your sister to try on the dress I've almost finished. Meanwhile, I'd better get back to what I was doing."

It wasn't more than a few minutes later when the two chatterboxes arrived, their cardigans draped over their shoulders in the mild early evening. Their talking ceased abruptly with the bang of the screen door behind them.

Nelson made an effort to appear deeply engrossed in Ernie Pyle's *Brave Men* but found the touching accounts of real-life wartime heroes far too moving for now. So he merely stared at the pages, occasionally turning one in pretense.

"Hi, Nelse," Stella said airily.

"Sis," he returned, looking up. "Hello, Mary."

The visitor offered a shy smile.

His heart thudded to a stop. Not only was she *as* beautiful as he'd first thought, but even *more,* if that were possible. Yet there seemed something far beyond her mere outward appearance that called out to his spirit whenever she was near. Something that made him think maybe he should try to help her, after all. All the more reason to focus his eyes on Ernie's book. Before he'd made sense out of the top paragraph, however, his mother reappeared, greeting the girls with her usual enthusiasm.

"Oh, Stella," she continued in a breathless rush, "supper won't be ready for a little while. Could you try on that new dress I've been working on? I'm sure your brother can keep Mary entertained for five minutes. I shouldn't need longer than that to mark the hem. Would you mind, Dear?"

Not entirely sure to whom she'd addressed the last question, Nelson shot her a glance.

"Sure, Mom," his sister answered. Then she turned to her

friend. . .who stood frozen, her eyes wide with fright. "I hope you don't mind, Mare. I'll be back in a jiffy." Showing her to the couch, she leveled a glower on Nelson. "And *you,* big brother, be your old charming self. Mary has yet to see that side of you."

My charming self, he thought with chagrin as his sister and their mother retreated to the sewing room off the kitchen.

Almost directly across from him now, Mary Theresa perched poker straight, her ankles crossed, her hands together in her lap, studiously refraining from glancing in his direction. Then her gaze drifted to the coffee table, where his mom's frayed Bible remained from this morning's reading.

An audible span of seconds ticked by on the mantel clock, a poignant silence which hung in the air between them.

He cleared his throat. "I've. . .uh. . .worked up a little song and dance routine," he began, "in case an awkward moment ever came along. . . ."

Her lips parted in obvious confusion, and her eyes hesitantly met his, as if she couldn't decide whether she should laugh.

Nelson flashed his best smile and his most offhanded shrug. "Best joke I could come up with. Sorry." A wave of relief washed over him as surprise skimmed across her face.

She held his gaze for a flicker of a moment, then lowered her eyes. "It—it was not what I expect. To make the joke."

"Little wonder," he admitted, "considering what a boor I was last time you were here. I hope I didn't offend you."

"No. You did not. I. . .understand."

"Know what? I think you probably do." He paused. "But if it's all the same to you, I'd like to apologize, anyway. And this evening I will try to be charming, like my baby sister advised."

Mary brightened, relaxing even more. "A good friend, Estelle is. Big help when first I start job."

Watching Mary as she spoke, Nelson noted the way her attention inevitably returned to the Bible in front of her—and lingered with an almost tangible yearning. "It's Mom's," he said quietly.

Those lovely turquoise eyes turned to his in question.

"The Bible. I noticed you admiring it."

She pinkened slightly. "It looks. . .loved," she murmured.

Nelson perused the leather-covered volume lying on the coffee table between them, realizing that the term he would probably have used to describe his mother's Bible was *worn out*. But now, seeing it through Mary's eyes, it took on a whole different quality. "It is that," he agreed. "Mom reads it morning and night, and whenever else she finds time. She's done that as far back as I can remember. Lately, she's started memorizing the Psalms."

"Many Psalms are there?"

The question caught him off guard. From her apparent interest, he'd expected her to be more familiar with God's Word. "A hundred and fifty," he explained. "So she's got a big task ahead."

"Someone else I once met knew much Bible," she said, her breathless voice so soft Nelson had to strain to hear it. "She would read to us, tell us. . .things."

"Us?"

But before she could explain, Stella and Mom breezed back into the parlor, which appeared to relieve Mary greatly.

His sister went immediately to their guest and plopped down on the arm of the sofa beside her. "I am so sorry, Mare, to leave you here with our resident grump. I hope he hasn't dragged you into his bad mood."

Nelson hiked his brows. "I'll have you know Mary and I got along just fine without you. Between us, we've managed to solve all the world's problems since the dawn of time."

"I can imagine." His sister's chin flattened in disdain. "Well, I've come to rescue her, anyway, so you can go back to whatever you were doing before we came home." Rising, she offered Mary a hand.

"As you wish," he answered facetiously, but the impish grin faded as he looked up at their visitor. "Maybe we can talk again sometime, Mary Theresa, about things."

꙳

Following Estelle to the second floor to freshen up, Mary drew what felt like her first real breath since arriving at the Thomas house. In her wildest imaginings, she wouldn't have pictured herself being left alone with her friend's brother for any length of time. Nor would she have expected to maintain a calm appearance. But, amazingly, Nelson had managed to put her at ease. . .at least on the surface. Underneath, she had been as jittery as her sewing machine's vibrations.

He seemed so different from the way he'd been last time she'd come. So much more pleasant and *likable*. But being a part of this family, how could he be otherwise?

But you must not grow fond of him, her wiser side lectured. *You must not even think of becoming close to any man.*

"So," Estelle said, as the two of them sank down on the patchwork quilt covering her single bed, "what did you and Nelse talk about all that time?"

"Mostly he talks. I listen."

Her friend giggled. "That's my brother, all right. Hey, we have a few minutes before Dad comes home and calls everyone to supper. You can be first to wash up, if you like."

As Mary walked down the hall to the bathroom, the few moments of solitude felt strangely like a reprieve. Any minute now, and she'd find herself across the table from Estelle's handsome brother. . .the young man who was becoming *friendly*. . . the young man who was starting to make her believe there could one day be restoration for her shattered trust.

His lips made music of her name. She knew better than to assign too much importance to something so simple as that, yet he made it sound so. . .intimate. Meeting her flushed reflection in the mirror above the sink, she splashed cool water on her face.

And he wanted the two of them to talk again. About things. Well, should the unlikely occasion ever arise, she would allow him to talk all he wanted. But she wasn't about to let the conversation revolve to her. Once this kind family discovered the kind of girl their daughter had befriended, Mary would no longer be welcome in their home.

Besides, even if she did allow herself to become interested in Nelson, what purpose would it serve? He couldn't possibly want her. No man would ever want her.

No, she had no plans of revealing her secrets. Not to Estelle, and especially not to Nelson.

six

"Would you care for another slice, Mary, dear?" Mrs. Thomas asked, the pastry server poised in readiness. "We wouldn't want you to leave the table hungry."

Mary's glance made a quick circuit around the loving Thomas household. Having polished off three entire meat pies, none of them could possibly still be hungry, least of all her. "No, thank you. Is full I am. Very good are the pasties."

"Why, thank you," the kind mother beamed, pleasure pinkening her button nose.

"I knew you'd like them," Estelle said. "Mom's are better than anyone's. She makes the flakiest crust around."

"Far be it from me to disagree," her father added pleasantly, patting his stomach. His thick brows arched higher, toward the receding hairline of his wavy, graying hair. "It's a favorite meal in this house."

"I second that," Nelson said with a nod. "They were great, Mom."

Feeling increasingly at ease around Estelle's parents, Mary astonished herself by voicing a favorite. "As child I loved *holubki,* stuffed cabbage. To have that I sometimes wish." Then, regretting having drawn attention to herself, she quickly sipped water from her glass, hoping she hadn't initiated a barrage of personal questions.

Mrs. Thomas sat forward in her chair at the foot of the table, hazel eyes alight. "Stuffed cabbage? Is it made with ground beef and rice? Tomato sauce?"

Mary nodded. "Yes."

A satisfied smile plumped her rosy apple cheeks, and she

sat up straighter, evening out the bib of the apron protecting her cross-stitched gingham housedress. "Well, isn't that interesting? I happen to make that dish myself. I just wasn't aware it had a foreign name. I'll prepare some next time you come to supper."

"Hey," Nelson cut in, "this is swell. More of the foods I missed out on when I was in the army." A grin as teasing as a summer breeze added a glimmer to his light brown eyes. "Any other delectable delights you have a hankering for, Mary?"

"What is served now I am liking," she said, stifling a maddening blush before it could make an appearance. It was ridiculous that he should affect her so.

"Well," Mr. Thomas said, unwittingly coming to her rescue, "let's put the icing on this tasty meal." He reached around to the maple buffet behind him for the book of Scripture readings. . .another delight she hungered for.

❧

Nelson watched Mary Theresa's face while his father read the evening devotional selection, a collage of verses pertaining to humility. *A person would have to be blind to miss that deep yearning,* he realized. When had he last savored—or even paid much attention to—Bible passages that were so familiar to him that he'd taken them for granted most of his life? He'd owned a variety of Bibles since he was a young boy, the latest version being a classy, gold-edged Scofield edition his parents gave him the Christmas before he'd gone off to the army. But it had gathered so much dust since he'd come home from rehab, he'd finally put it inside the drawer of his nightstand to assuage his guilt. He couldn't remember the last time he'd opened it.

Or the last time he'd prayed, for that matter.

He'd prayed his head off in battle, with mortar rounds and shrapnel exploding around him. . .right up until a shell came along that had his name on it. His and army buddy Mike Parsons's. Mike had died instantly. That's when Nelson decided nobody was listening to all those heavenly petitions.

He could still hear the chaplain mouthing platitudes to him until the medics arrived to put his writhing, agonized body on a stretcher. Could still remember the torture of the bumping, jostling military ambulance ride, endless miles while his leg blazed with a fire no one could put out. . .except the surgeons at the field hospital.

Those docs put the fire out, all right.

Permanently.

And from there he got a free ride home to America. To get *rehabilitated*. Man, how he hated that word.

❧

" 'If I then, your Lord and Master, have washed your feet,' " Mr. Thomas read, " 'ye also ought to wash one another's feet. For I have given you an example, that ye should do as I have done to you.' "

The passage relating to the humility of Jesus had perplexed Mary since her days in the concentration camp. It seemed an incredible concept then, and still did, to think that the very Son of God had not considered Himself above such a menial task, but performed it with the deepest love. The Prince of Heaven, with a servant's heart, as the Dutch woman would have said. Even as the priceless picture warmed Mary's insides, her glance drifted idly across the table to Nelson.

Apparently lost in a world of his own, an expression of intense bitterness had turned the young man's features as hard as granite. The sight stunned her. Before supper, he had seemed at ease and quite witty, and during the meal he injected the conversation with a steady stream of humor. He'd been fine until the ensuing Scripture reading. What could possibly have caused such a change?

Just then his gaze connected with hers, and the severity in

his facial planes vanished almost instantly.

Which baffled her even more.

"Well, Son," Mr. Thomas began, "we might find the Dodgers or Yankees playing somewhere on the radio if we turn the dial a bit. What say we get out of here and let the ladies do what ladies do best?" He eased his chair back and got up, pausing momentarily as if giving Nelson a chance to speak if he needed help. Then the two took their leave.

Mrs. Thomas immediately began clearing the table.

"Mom, you've worked enough today," Estelle reminded her. "Mare and I are more than capable of cleaning up. Sit down and relax for a change."

"Well. . ." After a slight hesitation she gave in. "Maybe I'll see if your father would like to go sit outside for awhile. There might not be a game on, after all."

Mary greatly appreciated yet another opportunity to visit with Estelle during the cleanup. Then, once the kitchen had been restored to order, they sought the comfort of the parlor, where they found Nelson at the card table working on a picture puzzle.

He motioned with his dark head toward the front steps without even looking up. "Mom and Dad are outside."

"We know," Estelle commented. "Want to join them, Mary?"

A knock rattled the screen door even as Estelle spoke, and she went to answer it. "Jon! Finished your shift, huh?"

"Sure did, Doll," came a low male voice. "Thought I'd drag that brother of yours out for a soda."

"Good luck!"

They both laughed.

"Well, come in," Estelle went on. "There's someone I'd like you to meet, even if you aren't able to pry Nelse out of here."

Mary's nerves started up immediately at the thought of being in the presence of yet another stranger as the tall, loose-jointed young man with sandy hair accompanied Estelle into the parlor's warm lamplight. He lifted an arm in greeting to Nelson before his attention turned in her direction.

"Jon," Estelle gestured, "this is Mary Malinowski, a friend of mine from Olympic. Mary, Jonathan Gray, Nelson's best buddy. He lives down the street a couple of houses."

"How do you do, Mary?" he said, an appraising smile on his long face. The blue checks in the cotton shirt he wore mirrored the hue of his eyes. Eyes that seemed keenly observant in their perusal.

Automatically, she inched back a fraction for more space. "Pleased to meet you," she whispered, wishing he would at least look away.

He kept up the assessment. "So you work with Stella, eh?"

Mary nodded.

"Good, good. She needs somebody to keep her in line."

Not completely sure what that meant, Mary manufactured as much of a smile as she could, then checked her watch.

"Oh!" Estelle gasped. "I almost forgot. It's time for me to walk you to the trolley stop."

"Need company?" Jon winked at Estelle.

She tilted her head a little, as if trying to decide. "Seeing as how you're a policeman, we probably should accept—but no. I've never heard of a problem on our street. We'll be safe enough."

An alarm shot through Mary at the thought of police escorting her anywhere. She reminded herself that this was America, and law enforcement officers were not to be feared. But not until she'd bid Mr. and Mrs. Thomas good-bye and she and Estelle had walked to the end of her block did she truly feel at ease.

"Jon's a really great guy," her friend gushed while they walked toward the nearest trolley stop.

"And interested in you," Mary pointed out. "I see him watching."

She brushed off the suggestion. "Nah, not really. He knows no one will ever measure up to—" Moistening her lips, Estelle swallowed without finishing the remark.

"About boyfriends we never talk," Mary said, her voice gentle. "A person so nice, like you, must have many."

Estelle craned her neck to peer down the cross street they had reached, but no streetcar was in sight. She turned and met Mary's eyes. "I was engaged, once. My high school sweetheart. The two of us thought we had our whole future planned. But with the war on, he entered the navy, not wanting to 'tie me down,' as he put it, until after the conflict was over. Only. . .his ship was torpedoed and sunk. No one made it off alive."

"I am sorry," Mary whispered. "I should not pry."

"So," Estelle continued, the forced cheerfulness in her voice a little obvious, "that's why Jon doesn't pester me. He knew my fiancé. . .most everybody in our neighborhood knows everybody else. I'm kind of glad he treats me like a sister, actually. It's all I need. Maybe someday I'll change my mind, but for now it's just fine." She drew a long slow breath, then exhaled. "Best of all, Jon keeps after Nelse as much as he can, trying to get him to get out of the house, but my stubborn brother's being a real stick-in-the-mud."

"Great pain, Nelson has," Mary said quietly. "Inside."

Estelle studied her in the glow of the street lamps. "Well, I sure wish he'd get over it. Very few families in this country came through the war without some personal loss along the way, including me. And we've all tried everything we know to help him. The worst thing is, he won't even come to church— and he used to be there whenever the doors opened, taking part. Now, though, the least little thing, and he's morbid as a graveyard."

Unsure of how to respond, Mary held her silence.

"Funny," Estelle said with a little frown, "he seemed in

pretty good spirits earlier, when the two of you talked, while Mom was marking the hem of my new dress."

Mary shrugged, not knowing what to say.

"Well, maybe Jon can knock some sense into him for real. Sometimes I think that's what it's gonna take."

Giving the dark-haired girl's arm an empathetic squeeze, Mary wished she could think of something terribly wise to impart. But all she could hear was Corrie ten Boom encouraging the women prisoners to support each other and help anyone else who bore scars from war, whether inside or out.

She just had serious doubts about being the one to help Estelle's brother.

"Well," Mary ventured, "if not keeping company with boyfriend, maybe some weekend you have free time."

Estelle's piquant face came alive with pleasure. "I have free time every weekend!"

"Then, some shopping we do?" Mary tried not to seem too hopeful. "My apartment. It is—American word—boring. Some pictures I want. Plants. Things to make pretty."

"Oh, that would be fun! I would love to!" Estelle nibbled her lip in thought. "Would you mind if I come over sometime this week to get an idea about what kinds of things you might be able to use?"

"Sure. I make chicken noodle soup for us."

"Super. Well, let's see. I have church and choir tomorrow night, but Thursday's free. Would that be okay with you?"

"Fine. Thursday." The very thought cheered Mary no end. Company at her place, two nights from now. And two more after that, a whole day at the stores with Estelle. What could be better?

The wheeze and rumble of an approaching streetcar drew her out of her imaginings. Meeting her friend's smile, she leaned to give her a hug. "Such fun I have, knowing you. Thank you for supper."

"You're quite welcome. I'll see you tomorrow," Estelle responded.

"Bright and early," they both said in unison, and giggled.

Thoughts of the enjoyable evening with Estelle's family kept Mary from feeling her usual loneliness on the homeward ride. She mulled over the events again and again, remembering the delicious meal, the comforting Scripture, the wonderful oneness of the home.

But the conversation with Nelson she tucked into a different place in her heart, one she wasn't entirely sure she should visit. She'd be better off not encouraging him to talk at all. At least, not to her. She had enough pain of her own to deal with.

seven

"Wow! What a dish," Jonathan exclaimed after Stella and Mary took their leave. "Gotta get me a job at a sewing factory." He moved closer to the window, hands in his pockets, gawking up the street at the girls.

Nelson cast an unbelieving gaze toward the ceiling.

Jon caught the snide look as he swung around and crossed the room. "Come on, Man. Any guy can see she's a looker, silky blond hair, incredible eyes. . ."

"Yeah, unless he happened to be blind. But Mary Theresa's got a lot more going for her than just that gorgeous face. She happens to be a very sensitive person."

"Ah, now." Jonathan bent to Nelson's level, a knowing grin spreading from ear to ear. "Do I detect a slight note of interest here?"

A slight note of interest? It seemed the more Nelson tried to keep his thoughts from wandering to Mary, the less successful he was at it. But even he knew the pointlessness of entertaining any grand daydreams. He branded his friend with a scowl. "No. You're way off base, Pal. Anyway, I thought you were carrying the torch for Stella."

"Let's say I'm biding my time." Straightening, Jon slid his hands back into his trouser pockets and rocked back on his heels. "And no fair changing the subject. We were talking about Mary. How long have you known her?"

Expelling a weary breath, Nelson rattled off the details, his tone flat as a phonograph record. "She's a friend of Stella's who comes for supper now and then. But I'm not interested— in her or anyone else." A corner of his lip curled in disdain.

"As if any dame would be desperate enough to want to be seen with a gimp."

Jon plopped his tall frame down to lounge on the couch, his long legs stretched out in front of him. "That's the sappiest thing that's ever come out of your mouth."

"You don't say. Well, it didn't take Nancy long to dump me when she got wind of my little mishap, did it? And she was supposed to love me forevermore, wasn't she?" Feigning indifference, Nelson returned his attention to the half-finished jigsaw puzzle, making an elaborate pretense of finding a particularly elusive piece.

Several uncomfortable minutes ticked by before Jon emitted a disgusted whoosh of air and stood. "Well, it doesn't appear you're in the mood for company tonight. I only came over here in the first place to see if you wanted to go for a ride in my new jitney."

Nelson perked up. "You got yourself a car?"

"Yeah. Well, okay, so it's not much to brag about—yet. Only set me back a hundred and fifty clams. But I figure I can knock out the dents in my spare time. Then, a coat of paint, and she'll be almost good as new."

Forgetting his aversion to leaving the house, Nelson lumbered to a standing position, unmindful of a few puzzle pieces that fell to the floor in the process. "This I gotta see."

"Well, well," Jon mused. "If I'd have known a bucket of bolts would be all it took to get you out of here, I'd have sprung for one months ago."

Nelson grabbed his crutches. "Just shut up and lead the way."

Outside, he gave his friend's '34 Ford Roadster the once-over, from the greyhound hood ornament to the whitewalled spare tire mounted above the back bumper. Though the flashy little vehicle showed its age, he could see obvious possibilities. The interior looked more than reasonable. He blew out a silent whistle. "Rumble seat and all, eh?"

"Yep." The word barely concealed the pride in Jon's voice. "And peppy. She's got a Flathead V-8. Belonged to one of the guys at the precinct, but his wife just had twins a couple months ago, so they needed something bigger. Course, it took me awhile to convince him of that," he said with a wink.

"Well, let's see what she can do." Nelson opened the door and eased himself inside, one hand still on his crutches as he inhaled the enticing smells particular to cars. Leather and grease and. . .adventure.

"Here, let me run those sticks up to the house," Jon offered. "I can grab 'em again when we get back."

On his return, he wasted no time in folding down the convertible top. "Might as well get the full effect," he said, his grin just shy of gloating. Taking the driver's seat, he started the engine and maneuvered the knob-handled gearshift into low, and tooted a jaunty "Aooogah" to Nelson's parents. When he pulled out onto the street, he headed westward.

This is the life, Nelson thought, reveling in the engine's purr, the feel of the wind tossing his hair in wild abandon as miles sped by, apartment buildings and shops on one side, and the dark waters of the Hudson River on the other. *Too bad my little black coupe has been sitting and gathering rust since I went away. I should sell the thing and give Dad the money, since I'm never gonna use it.*

"How 'bout a soda?" Jon asked, turning to him. "I need some gas." Without waiting for a response, he pulled into a Texaco station just ahead on the right and nodded to the skinny, pimply attendant. "Fill 'er up, kid."

While the boy pumped the fuel and washed the windshield, Jonathan strode inside the station and emerged with two nickel bottles of carbonated soda pop. He handed one to Nelson before starting off again.

Neither spoke for a short span until Jon braked for a traffic light. "Did you mean what you said back home, Nelse?" he asked. "About being a gimp?" He gulped several swallows of his drink.

"Well, what would *you* call a one-legged cripple?" Nelson groused.

"You don't have to be a cripple unless you wanna be," his friend chided. "So what if you have part of a leg missing? They did fit you with an artificial limb at rehab, didn't they?"

"Yeah. Right. Super deluxe model, flexible ankle joint, the whole bit. Smooth and shiny as a brand-new penny. Even wears one of my shoes."

"So, where is it?"

Nelson glowered at him. "In the closet. The stupid thing hurts my stump."

"It wouldn't once you got used to it. I know other guys who—"

"Look. Lay off, will you?" he railed. "I don't wanna talk about it. I'm tired, anyway. Let's head back."

"Okay, okay." Jonathan raised a hand in defense, a muscle working in his jaw as he clamped his mouth shut. But he didn't remain quiet for long. "But I might as well tell you this, as a friend, before you hear it from somebody else. I'm glad you didn't end up with Nancy Belvedere. She was messing around with Ray Baxter, down at the precinct, while you were off earning Bronze Stars and Purple Hearts. You deserve a whole lot better gal than her, anyway."

That piece of news floored Nelson. Could his fiancée really have been making a patsy out of him behind his back? He'd never once doubted her love. On the other hand, he'd never known Jonathan to lie, either. The two of them went back a lifetime. But forcing his thoughts in a different direction during the oppressive silence as they motored homeward, the nagging truth of his friend's admonition regarding the replacement limb wouldn't let Nelson alone. It was his own fault he'd never become accomplished at walking with the thing. He hadn't been one to spend a lot of time practicing. Before, everything physical had always come easily. A little too easily. Maybe he should dig out that ugly contraption, give it another shot.

ༀ

"Let's run to Woolworth's for some lunch," Estelle suggested. "All this shopping has me starved."

Enjoying the beautiful Saturday, Mary Theresa nodded in agreement. The endless variety of merchandise available in American department stores never ceased to amaze and delight her. Having checked the newest designs in home fashion at Macy's and Gimbel's, she'd chosen only a few small items she could not resist, knowing the less expensive wares of the five-and-ten would be more within her means.

Their purchases firmly in hand, the two of them exited the main entrance to the bustling thoroughfare, then headed straight to the popular dime store, where they took stools at the lunch counter, paying no mind to shoppers browsing only a few feet away.

While her friend perused a menu from the chrome holder in front of them, Mary Theresa scanned the daily specials displayed on a small chalkboard. "Good. Today is hot roast beef sandwich. That I get," she told the slim, redheaded waitress. "And please, a glass of water."

"I think I'll have the grilled cheese," Estelle decided, "with potato chips and a lemonade."

With a crack of her chewing gum, the freckled girl gave a nod and went to fill their orders.

Mary feasted on her meal when it arrived, especially the mound of mashed potatoes with brown gravy. It tasted a little bit of home. The Old Country.

"I think we've done pretty well so far, don't you?" Estelle commented before biting into the second half of her sandwich. "Those utensils in the rotating stand will look cute on your counter. And the matching towels and hot pads from Gimbel's will brighten that little kitchenette."

"Yes. Very pretty they are. But still I must find pictures to hang. Such plain walls." With a rueful shake of her head, Mary polished off the rest of her roast beef, increasingly eager to survey every remaining inch of Woolworth's store.

A few hours and a fair amount of money later, the two of them emptied their purchases in a heap on Mary Theresa's couch, draped their sweaters across its arm, and kicked off their shoes.

"The pictures I want to hang first," Mary declared, sorting through the stack for the framed pastels she'd chosen. Then her shoulders sagged. "Oh, no! A hammer we forget."

"Not necessarily," Estelle said with a smile. "I knew you wanted to spruce up your walls, so I tucked Mom's steak pounder and some tacks into my purse, just in case."

Mary seized the girl's slender frame in a hug. "Too much, you are. Thank you. Now we must get busy. This picture of wishing well and butterflies I think for over there, don't you?"

Long after they finished, had supper, and Estelle had gone home, Mary Theresa couldn't bring herself to turn off the light. Midnight was fast approaching, and she felt bone weary after the busy day, but she couldn't stop admiring their handiwork. What a difference homey touches like colorful throw pillows, inexpensive figurines, philodendron plants, and sheer curtain panels made in her little place. It looked almost. . .reborn.

With her heart filled to bursting, Mary Theresa slipped to her knees. She could think of no prayer from her years of catechism which could begin to express her deep gratitude, yet she sensed that the good things which had happened to her came from God. But how could she dare to approach Him in the familiar style some people had adopted?

People like Corrie ten Boom and the Thomases were naturally good, Mary reasoned. Like saints. They hadn't participated in the abominable acts she'd been subjected to at Ravensbruck. How could she expect a holy God to hear the innermost prayers of someone like her, someone so unworthy?

A fruitless wish rose to taunt her. If only she were pure, like Estelle and the Chudzik daughters. But the vile past could never be undone, and its black shroud bowed her shoulders with an oppressive weight of guilt and shame she could never forget.

God loves us all, she could hear Corrie admonish. *No matter how unworthy you may feel, He knows your heart. Each of you is precious in His sight. He wants you to come to Him. He is watching for you and waiting for you to come.*

Hoping that were true, longing for it to be true, Mary clasped her hands before her and swallowed the lump of apprehension clogging her throat. "Thank You, dear God," she whispered. "Thank You." Her prayer couldn't begin to express what she felt, but with her whole being she harbored the hope that it would somehow please Him.

eight

"Whatever possessed me to wear my new shoes to work?" Estelle wailed after the trolley's doors whooshed shut and the conveyance pulled away. "I should have saved them for church. I just know I have a huge blister."

Accompanying her limping coworker home for what had evolved into a weekly get-together with Estelle's family, Mary slipped an arm around her. "Slow we walk. Not so much hurt."

Estelle gave a pained smile when they turned down her street. "They looked so stylish in the store window on Saturday. That's what I get for buying in haste." Suddenly she stopped. "Wait, this should help more than anything." Placing a hand on Mary's shoulder for balance, she slipped both shoes and anklets off entirely, revealing an angry, nickel-sized abrasion on one foot. "Mmm, much better." But tiny lines of distress fanned out from her eyes as she gingerly walked the rest of the way barefooted.

Even Mary was glad when they finally reached the portion of the tenement row house belonging to the Thomases. They mounted the steps and went inside.

"Well, well," Nelson remarked in the entry, grinning like the Cheshire cat in Christine Chudzik's favorite story. "Olympic's star seamstresses return home after a hard day at the factory."

Estelle just groaned and headed for the couch, where she collapsed with a sigh onto the slipcovered cushions.

But Mary had detected a decidedly cheerier tone than usual in Nelson's voice and glanced up at him. Then she realized something else. He seemed taller than she remembered.

70

Why, he was standing! Without crutches! An unbidden smile of astonishment teased her lips.

"Thought it was high time I mastered the old peg leg," he quipped with a self-conscious shrug. "They say all it takes is practice, practice, and more practice. Either of you gals up to a little stroll around the block?" He looked from one to the other in speculation.

"Count me out," Estelle moaned. "It was all I could do to stroll home, with this swell blister I acquired, compliments of my new shoes."

"Mary Theresa?" he asked tentatively, dark, even brows climbing to his mahogany hair in question. "I gotta warn you, though. I'm not very good at this yet, so I could very likely trip over one or both of my feet. . .in case you'd rather not risk the embarrassment of being seen with a clumsy oaf."

His poignant smile tore at her heart. In truth, Mary would have preferred to remain behind with Estelle. . .but not for the reason he suggested. Her aversion related to being alone with men—period. Still, the fact that Nelson was more concerned with her possible discomfort than his own struck a tender note in her spirit. He'd never given her cause not to trust him. And he looked so vulnerable, wobbling ever so slightly while he waited for her response. How could she refuse?

"Sure thing. I go. There is time?" she asked as he reached around to push the screen door open for her.

"Oh, you mean before supper. Yeah, Dad hasn't come in yet. Besides, I probably can't walk very far." Following her outside, Nelson stopped and turned, poking his head back inside. "Sis? Tell Mom we won't be too long, okay?" He let the door close with a bang.

Mary went down the steps first, then stood aside, trying not to show her alarm as he tackled the same feat, his movements haltingly slow and ungainly, his face scrunched up in concentration.

When he made it to the sidewalk, he flashed a toothy grin. "See? Easy as pie."

She couldn't suppress a smile. "This I see."

Letting him set the pace, Mary did her best to stay out of the way, yet remained close enough to offer assistance, just in case. The coming evening was sure to be a lovely one, with the mild ocean breeze gently stirring the treetops, occasionally tugging stray hairs loose from their pins. She let her gaze drift to the assortment of row homes on either side of the street, noticing the lamplight beginning to glow here and there behind the curtained windows. A sprinkle of children's laughter added a charm of its own.

"It's been pretty nice having you come to supper with Stella," Nelson said between grunts as he hobbled along. "She's been needing a friend. Most of her schoolmates are married now and busy with their own lives."

"Good for me, too, she is. Only my host family I know—and yours—in America."

"Did you come from a large family back in Poland?"

A twinge of alarm skittered up Mary's spine, but at the sincerity in his voice, she willed her wariness aside. "Two brothers, one sister, our parents." Speaking of her departed loved ones didn't sting as much as she'd expected, though she knew the sadness would never completely go away.

"I'd like to hear about them someday," Nelson said, "when you feel like talking."

Mary slanted him a glance, noticing how the brown plaid shirt deepened his eyes to a rich chocolate shade. "Perhaps. Someday."

He smiled then, a smile slow and gentle and filled with understanding.

She stifled a gasp as the world came to a sudden standstill.

Turning the next corner, Nelson stumbled. His hands flailed madly about, finally latching onto Mary in a desperate move to keep from falling.

She tamped down a rush of unwelcome memories and held her ground until he'd regained his balance.

"Sorry," he murmured, abashed as he released his grip. "Please forgive me. I was stupid to attempt this without a cane."

Still fighting for her own composure, Mary tried to ignore the lingering traces of his touch. Amazingly, she felt strangely bereft as they faded away—despite her loathsome experiences at the concentration camp. "Home you have the cane?" she blurted out. "I could get it."

Guilt colored Nelson's strong features as he shook his head. "I broke the fool thing, over my good knee. Pretty dumb, now that I think about it."

He had the most disarming way of making her smile, Mary realized. And she shouldn't be smiling. "Are you hurt?" she finally managed, subduing the uncustomary giddiness she so often felt in his presence. . .even as her practical side reminded her there could never be anything more than friendship between them.

"Naw. Except for my pride." Nelson started forward again, and she fell into step beside him. "At one time I was quite the athlete," he went on candidly. "Played football in high school; ran track for the sheer fun of it." He paused. "I thought my life was over when I found out I was a cr—I mean, lost my leg. For several months in the hospital, I was furious at the doctors for pulling me through."

"Some people were not so fortunate," Mary whispered, her eyes fixed on the sidewalk.

❧

The quiet reminder sliced through Nelson's conscience. Here he was, strong and healthy and walking around—however clumsily—in two shoes. While beside him was an angel-spirited beauty who'd had her whole family senselessly ripped away, yet she gave no murmur or complaint. What right did he have to gripe? Or more important, to blame God? Estelle had been right. So was Jon, and so was Mary. It was time he smartened up.

"Thanks." He looked at her with a half-smile. "For the reminder, I mean."

She lowered her lashes and kept the slow, laborious pace.

By the time they turned the final corner and were nearing home, Nelson's stump ached. He should have been content just to go to the corner and back on his first try, instead of overdoing things.

But he wouldn't have missed this walk for anything.

Enticing supper smells met them as he and Mary climbed the steps and went inside.

"Oh, good," his mom said. "Everything's ready. Soon as you two come to the table, we can eat."

❧

"How is blister?" Mary Theresa asked as she took her place next to Estelle.

She gave her an agonized look. "The same. Sure hope I can find some comfortable shoes to wear to work tomorrow."

"I hope, too."

Mr. Thomas waited until he had everyone's attention, then folded his hands and bowed his head. "We thank You, dear Lord, for Your wondrous provisions. Thank You for bringing our Mary back to us for another evening. Please continue to keep Your hand of blessing upon her day by day. And please touch Stella's foot and ease the discomfort she's feeling. Help us to be faithful to You always. Now bless this food so lovingly prepared for us all, in the name of your precious Son. Amen."

Once again, Mary was touched by the prayer—and by the amazing concept that Almighty God would concern Himself with such trivial matters as blisters! Such a spirit of love pervaded this home, this family, she found herself counting the days until she could be here again. *Our Mary,* Estelle's father had called her. And heaven help her, she truly wished she were a part of them.

But she knew that could never be. Christians or not, some things simply could not be shared with these dear people. She couldn't bear the look she knew would be in their eyes. To be precious in God's eyes, that would have to be enough for her.

"Help yourself, Dear," Mrs. Thomas said, passing the stuffed cabbage. "I hope it's the way you like it."

Shaking off the cruel reality which had dampened her pleasant reverie, Mary smiled and took the bowl. "Delicious, it looks. Like back in Poland."

"Mom even made bread today," Estelle commented. "Since it goes so well with the dish."

"Enough chatter," Nelson teased. "There's a couple of hungry men waiting for the food to come our way."

Estelle tossed her thick hair and gave a mock salute. "Yes, Sir! Right away, Sir!" After placing two cabbage rolls on her plate, she passed the bowl to her father.

"How was the walk, Son?" the older man asked, his expression colored by a mixture of surprise and satisfaction. He nudged his bifocals a bit higher.

"Not too bad. Mary Theresa only had to carry me the last stretch." Filling his own plate, Nelson winked at her.

Mary decided she'd better give her whole concentration to the task of buttering the fresh, cloudlike bread.

After the meal ended, she helped her hostess clear the table while Estelle elevated her sore foot.

"I'm so happy to have you to supper with us," Mrs. Thomas said, putting on her apron and removing a second from the drawer for Mary.

"This I not need," she tried to protest.

But the older woman wouldn't be dissuaded. "No sense

spoiling that pretty dress," she insisted, tying the strings snugly around Mary's waist, mothering her. "You have such lovely clothes."

Mary swallowed down a rush of emotion. "Thank you. Host family, the Chudziks, help me dress American."

"Well, they taught you well. Still, it can get quite warm here in the city in the summertime. You might consider some dresses with short sleeves. It's much cooler that way."

"Maybe new dresses I buy next summer," she placated, knowing the day would never come when she would expose those disgusting concentration camp identification numbers to the world.

"How long have you been in New York now?" Mrs. Thomas asked while the dishpan filled with water.

Mary fought to regain her serenity. "I think seven, maybe eight months."

"I do hope you like it here. There are lots of things to do in the city, places to go." She added dinner plates and glasses to the sudsy water.

"Yes. To museums the Chudziks are taking me sometimes. And parks."

"I'm glad. We really love having you here with us and would like to think you're happy in America."

Nodding, Mary reached for the first item set on the drain board. "Peace there is here. Not like back home. This I like. And your family."

With a teary smile and soapy hands, the little woman hugged her.

Not until the time came for Mary to leave did she remember that Estelle wouldn't be able to walk her to the trolley. Mary wasn't exactly fearful of navigating the streets at night, and it was only two blocks to the stop. Surely she could manage that short distance.

But Nelson lumbered to his feet as she headed for the door.

"Thought I'd keep you company."

"Safe I am. Truly. No need to come."

He raised a hand to quiet her protests. "I need all the practice I can get, remember?"

"Are you sure, Son?" Mr. Thomas asked from his customary parlor chair. "I could drive her home in my car."

"Yeah, Dad. I intend to walk as much as I possibly can."

Alarm jolted her heart, but what could she say? A quick good-bye to Estelle and her parents, and Mary again started up the street with the one young man in the world she knew she'd be wiser to avoid.

Nelson's gait was still quite awkward, and Mary sensed this walk caused him even more discomfort, but they had plenty of time before the next streetcar arrived.

When they finally gained the stop, Nelson reached inside the sweater he'd put on and drew out a book. "I have something for you. Sort of a thank you for putting up with a clumsy oaf. It's not much."

Mary took the volume he held out, its leather cover soft and flexible beneath her fingertips. "Oh!" she gasped. "A Bible it is! I cannot—"

"Yes, you can. It's not that great, Mary. Just my old one. It's pretty marked up and all, so I hope you don't mind. Mom and Dad bought me a new Bible not long ago. It's silly letting this collect dust on my bookshelf. And the way you seemed to admire Mom's. . .I'd like you to have it."

Fighting against a stinging behind her eyelids, Mary Theresa could barely utter a word. "Thank you," she somehow said around her tight throat.

When the night breeze tossed a stray lock of hair into her eyes, Nelson reached to brush it away, the touch of his fingertips warming her to her toes. The subdued light revealed a longing in his eyes that she'd never glimpsed before, and it changed the rhythm of her pulse.

The approaching trolley rumbled to a stop just then, and Nelson handed her up. "Good night, Mary Theresa."

She smiled past the mistiness in her eyes and stumbled blindly to a seat, silently voicing her thankfulness to God that the streetcar had come along when it had. . .because otherwise she might have kissed Nelson Thomas.

nine

Aware that she was beginning to nod off, Mary Theresa blinked and peered through heavy eyelids at the alarm clock beside her bed. Two A.M. already? But it was worth the loss of sleep. She closed the Bible Estelle's brother had given her and hugged it to her heart. *Thank You for granting my dearest wish.* Like a soul coming out of a famine, she'd already struggled through a portion of the New Testament, flipping through in search of familiar passages, laboring over the outdated English words, yet determined to conquer them.

She noticed that Nelson had underlined verses here and there, often with an addition of a written note or related reference along the margin in a neat, strong hand. Even though some of the comments were beyond her understanding, she still stopped to peruse them whenever she came to one, pondering new meanings and concepts.

So far, she admitted with a yawn, all seemed to coincide with the wonderful things Corrie ten Boom passed along to her and the other women at the death camp. And that only increased her hunger to know more.

"A new day is tomorrow." Then with supreme reluctance, she laid the treasured Book on her night table. A Bible all her own. No reason to hurry. She would read slowly, as her limited command of the language necessitated, starting with the Gospel of John, where she'd discovered the sewn-in ribbon marker had been placed. And she would savor every word.

Turning to her side, Mary snuggled into her pillow, her thoughts a delicious blend of Scripture verses and the evening stroll with Estelle's very charming brother. His voice still rang in her mind, and her heart skipped at the memory of the longing she'd seen in his eyes in that unguarded moment. Even yet, it reawakened yearnings she had buried long ago and never planned to resurrect.

Inside, she knew she should not dwell on even the smallest of such forbidden pleasures. But still. . .what could it hurt just to think about him for a little while, to imagine she was just like other young women, just for tonight. . .?

૨૦

Nelson rose from the upholstered chair when his parents came downstairs dressed for prayer meeting. "Thought I'd tag along this time—if you don't mind a slowpoke, that is." He'd practiced walking throughout the day and already could detect marginal improvement since those first two attempts last night with Mary Theresa. She'd been very enjoyable company, and he'd appreciated the opportunity of getting to know her a little. He'd never met anyone so shy. Something about her plucked an unplayed chord inside his spirit, though he still doubted that any woman could find him appealing, least of all someone as perfect as she. No, better to think of her as a friend and be grateful for that much.

Aside from that, he rather hoped for a chance to talk to the pastor after church.

A look of elation passed between the older couple before his dad grabbed him in a bone-crushing hug, wrinkling Nelson's best suit. "Remind me to thank Jon and Mary for whatever they did to get you to return to the land of the living," the older man teased.

"Hey, did I miss something?" Stella asked, straightening the waistband of her pleated charcoal skirt as she traipsed down from her room, a false pout on her lips. "I thought I heard someone mention Mary."

Mom just smiled. "Your father just commented on how indebted we are to that dear girl. Leave the parlor light on,

Nelson. I don't like coming home to a dark house."

Stella shot a glance to Nelson and placed a hand over her heart in pretend shock. "Don't tell me you have deigned to honor us with your presence at the Wednesday night service."

"Shut up, Squirt," he countered, purposely flicking a lock of her curly hair into her face.

Hardly offended by the brotherly prank, she wrinkled her nose at him and followed their parents out to their old four-door sedan, with Nelson lagging behind.

A reasonably short drive took them to the stately brick church a stone's throw from Central Park, where the older couple had met, married, and remained members in the ensuing years. Nelson couldn't have imagined his family going elsewhere.

"As I live and breathe," Pastor Herman said, striding to meet their little group when they entered the sanctuary a scant few minutes before the service. Of medium height with a wiry build, the man ran his long fingers through his thatch of white hair and headed straight to Nelson, a warm smile revealing perfect dentures. "Welcome back, young man. It's good to see you again. This is an answer to prayer."

"Yours and everybody else's," Nelson supplied with a droll grin while they shook hands. "Sorry it took so long."

"The Lord has all the time in the world, Son," he returned kindly, then greeted the rest of the family before turning his attention to Nelson once more. "You're with the rest of your 'family' now, my boy. A few of our brave servicemen didn't make it back from the war, I'm sad to say, but I'm sure you'll see some familiar faces. It's time to get started, so have yourself a seat, and I'll steer a couple folks your way after the service."

Only too happy to oblige, Nelson followed Stella, taking the spot between her and his mom, with his father occupying the aisle seat. After nodding and waving to a half-dozen individuals whose attention their arrival had roused, he let his gaze drink in the familiar painted and paneled surroundings, walnut pews and altar, high ceiling, and burgundy-carpeted aisles. A sight he'd sorely missed during the European conflict.

Before he'd chosen to study engineering, he often pictured himself occupying a similar pulpit, commanding the attention of a large congregation who hung on his every word. But those youthful dreams no longer held appeal. Now he was content just to listen to a man of God passing on the rich nuggets of truth gleaned from hours of study and prayer.

From the opening of the service, when the organist played "Shall We Gather at the River?" to the end of this installment in the minister's sermon series on the cross of Jesus as foretold throughout the Bible, Nelson sensed his spirit absorbing the presence of the Lord as a dry sponge soaked up water.

"So you see," the preacher said in conclusion, holding his open Bible aloft, "we have in Isaiah fifty-three yet another vivid word picture of our suffering Savior, one written hundreds of years before His birth in Bethlehem. From Genesis to Revelation, God has provided unmistakable portraits of His Son, the 'Lamb slain from the foundation of the world.' His wondrous plan for reconciling fallen man unto Himself is revealed from cover to cover throughout His holy Word. Let us bow in prayer."

Afterward, the congregation broke up into small groups to pray for the individual needs of the members and others. Nelson, however, caught the pastor's eye, and the white head tipped in the direction of his study, an invitation Nelson promptly accepted. He made his way there as quickly as his uneven gait would allow.

"What can I do for you, Son?" Pastor Herman closed the door behind them, gesturing toward an armchair facing his massive desk before taking the worn leather one behind it for himself.

The man's appearance, Nelson noted, was as neat and

orderly as the room had always been as far back as he could remember. Small things, yet they instilled trust and confidence. And those sharp blue eyes, though discerning, always put a person at ease. "I'm not sure. I just need to talk to somebody who doesn't live with me. Confess, maybe. That's supposed to be good for the soul."

"Quite. It's another example of obedience. The New Testament encourages us to confess our faults to one another."

"I understand." He paused. "I guess what I have to say is, it's finally gotten through my thick skull that I've been blaming God for letting me lose a leg, when I should have been thanking Him for saving my life. All these months I've been wallowing in self-pity. What a waste. I really need to make things right and start living for God again. Just wanted you to know."

A gentle smile appeared on the pastor's mouth. "It's very gratifying to hear that, Nelson. The folks here at church have been praying for you for a long time. I'd suggest you consider making your rededication public some Sunday, let them know their prayers have been answered."

"Thank you, Sir. You're right. I probably should do that." Limping down that long carpeted aisle while everyone watched would take some courage—and that he was starting to regain, thanks to Mary Theresa's willingness to help him practice. Had she opened and read the Bible he'd passed along to her? Would she search the pages until she found the peace she so needed?

The minister's smile widened into the grin Nelson remembered. "I'm real glad to have you back, Son." Rising, he came around the desk and clamped an encouraging hand on Nelson's shoulder.

❧

Mary Theresa gave her finished work a final count the following Tuesday, before returning it to the basket to be turned in.

"Another long, long day," Estelle commented, covering her

own machine. She placed a hand on her spine and arched her back a little. "Time for us to go home for supper."

"Getting tired of me your family must be," Mary said, expressing one of her fears.

"Not a chance. They look forward to having you eat with us every week. In fact, Mom and Dad have really taken to you. They talk about you as if you're their long-lost daughter—which is fine with me. I always wished I had a sister." Picking up her production quota, Estelle headed for the clerk's counter, the skirt of her floral print dress swaying.

And Nelson, Mary wanted to ask. *What about him? Does he speak of me, too?* She was eager to know how the walking was coming along, among other things. Spending much of her free time in his old Bible gave her a clearer picture of the man inside, and the deeply spiritual person he'd been before the war awed her. A large part of her envied that intimate relationship he'd had with God before he'd been severely wounded. Would he ever recover it? Would she ever find her way to her own peace? Expelling a breath, Mary leaned down for her basket, then followed her friend.

"Is everything okay with you, Mare?" Estelle asked over the rumble of the trolley on their way home. "You've been quiet for days."

Mary patted her friend's hand, noticing that she and Estelle both sported on their fingers the ever-present traces of pinpricks so common among sewing factory employees. "On my mind there is much. Every night, staying up late, reading, reading."

"Must be a swell book!"

"Yes. The Bible."

"Oh." Estelle seemed a bit taken aback for a second. "Well, if you come across anything puzzling, Nelson's a good one to ask. He usually knows the answer. At least, he always did before he left for the war. In our church's youth group, he was the captain of the quiz team, forever drilling everybody else in memory verses and Bible facts."

Interesting, Mary thought. But she really couldn't bother him with her trivial questions. She needed to put distance between them again, concentrate on her friendship with Estelle, as she had in the beginning.

"Thank goodness he finally started coming to church again," her friend continued. "He went with us last Wednesday night and twice last Sunday. I've even been seeing him studying his Scofield the way he used to."

That last bit of news filled Mary with unexpected joy. Up and around on his artificial leg, and back at church? Perhaps he truly had made his peace with God. "And you?" she probed. "In your room a Bible I see. Do you read every day?"

Estelle shifted in her seat, her cheeks taking on a pinkish hue. "I, um, don't always give it the time I should, I'm afraid."

"In Poland, no Bible I have," Mary said quietly. "The priests only have them. But I think, in country with so many Bibles, everybody read."

"Not as many as one might expect." Turning to her, Estelle spoke with candor. "I used to read through the Scripture from cover to cover every year. But when Ken, my fiancé, was killed, I hit a pretty low spot. After that, I didn't pick it up for ages."

"Yes," Mary agreed. "To part with loved one is not easy."

"I might have known you'd understand." She lowered her gaze to the worn floorboards. "I must admit, I questioned the purpose to life—all the while, seriously doubting there was one. Of course, I still went to church during those dark days. Heaven forbid my parents should see how weak their darling girl's faith was."

Mary nodded but didn't respond.

"Now," her friend babbled on, "I've gone back to reading through my Bible again. As far as delving into the heavy stuff, though, I kind of leave that to guys who want to be preachers." She flashed an embarrassed grin. "I know, I shouldn't feel that way. And my conscience has been niggling me about it. The Lord expects His followers to be able to provide answers regarding their faith."

Mary really wanted more than that. She wished Estelle would also provide more answers about her brother. But plying her with endless questions would hardly be wise. The man was already on Mary's mind a little too much. When she studied his Bible, it seemed she could hear his voice doing the reading. Somehow, that had to stop.

Arriving at the Thomases', she found Nelson looking comfortable and way too appealing in the easy chair by the radio, his legs propped on the matching hassock. His new black Bible lay open in his lap.

He glanced up with a smile as they disposed of their purses. "Hi, Sis. Hi, Mary. What's new?"

"New? At the salt mines?" His sister snickered. "You've got to be kidding."

Obviously unaffected, he switched his attention from her and zeroed in on Mary, a twinkle in his wide-set eyes. "How about you? Read any good books lately?"

"One only," Mary answered evenly, knowing he understood.

But Estelle filled in the blanks. "She's been reading the Bible. And I volunteered you, O knowledgeable one, to help her with all her questions."

Mary didn't know whether to blush or blanch, she had such a rush of anticipation, mixed with fear and embarrassment.

Nelson, however, displayed a mouthful of healthy teeth with his easy grin. "I was just about to go out for another daily constitutional—which, thanks to Dad, shouldn't be such a chore this time." Producing a cane from beside the chair, he waved it with a flourish. "Want to keep me company, Mary Theresa? Any questions you might have, just ask away."

Mary figured she'd probably come to regret spending more time with the object of so many of her wayward thoughts. But surely she had things in their proper perspective now. If she kept her focus on biblical questions only, maybe it would be all right. Or so she told herself. "Sure. I go."

ten

"That's quite the cloud bank rolling in off the ocean," Nelson commented upon reaching the sidewalk outside. "We've been needing a good rain."

Mary checked the sky, then matched his pace as they set out on their trip around the block. She immediately noticed a new smoothness in his steps now that he had the aid of a cane. Obviously, he had been practicing, and the extra effort showed. And she didn't mind admitting he looked wonderful, despite his limp. So manly and appealing as the slanted rays of the sun gilded the planes of his face.

With an inward sigh, she diverted her gaze to the row houses lining the road. A variety of delectable suppers emitted their mouth-watering smells into the early evening air, to be blended together occasionally by the breeze from a passing car. Any minute, and her stomach was sure to growl and embarrass her.

"So, you've been reading the Bible, eh?" Nelson asked casually.

Mary had wondered how and when he'd bring up the subject. "Yes."

"So have I, thanks to you."

The unexpected statement caught her by surprise. She swung a glance his way and saw a warm grin reflecting its glow in his light brown eyes. And for a precious few seconds, she imagined they were like any other couple out for a pleasant stroll.

His voice brought her back to earth. "Before you started coming home with Stella," he began, "I'd resigned myself to spending the rest of my days in that easy chair in our front room, feeling sorry for myself. I'd shut the Lord out of my life, feeling it was all His fault I'd lost a leg. He was supposed to take care of me, you see. Or so I believed. It took you to make me realize He really had looked out for me, after all."

A little unsure of his meaning, Mary gave him a questioning look.

"The shell that wounded me took my army buddy's life. It could have just as easily taken mine, too."

"Oh." Thinking of the raft of relatives and friends who had been wrenched out of her world, Mary Theresa had no trouble at all relating to his loss. "You lose the friend. That pain I know." She averted her gaze to a noisy group of children in the street who'd ceased their game of kick-the-can until she and Nelson passed.

"Somehow I doubt my losing one pal measures up to what you've gone through," he added, once they were beyond the range of activity.

Not about to illuminate him on that understatement, Mary stared straight ahead, content to let him do the talking. As long as he was the topic instead of her, she had no fears.

They turned the next corner, and Nelson resumed where he'd left off.

"Just knowing that you understand has helped me. Got me moving again, at long last."

"I am glad."

He stopped abruptly and turned to her. "By the way, Mary Theresa, I hope you don't mind me butting in between you and Stella. I know she's the reason you come over. I'll try not to monopolize you from now on. But I just wanted you to know I appreciate your letting me ramble on. It's like having another sister." He started forward again.

Rambling was the last thing Mary would have called the moving account he had just shared. . .but the "sister" part burst the tiny bubble she'd allowed to start growing in her dreams. She let out a stoical breath and caught up to Nelson. After all, she knew better than to dream in the first place.

As if sensing the change in atmosphere, Nelson reverted to the original subject. "Stella says you have some questions pertaining to the Bible?"

Mary relaxed and shrugged a shoulder. "Not a big question. Just a little one."

"And it's about. . ." he said, coaxing her on.

"The notes you are writing on the sides of the pages. Such as at the supper, when Jesus is washing the disciples' feet."

"Oh, yeah," he said with a wry grimace. "Sorry about all my scribbling. I should have gotten you a new Bible."

"No. The writing, this is fine," she quickly assured him. "Sometimes a big help, especially with English words I not understand."

He appeared to contemplate her statement for a moment. "Then what's the problem?"

She cocked her head back and forth, wondering how to put her thoughts into English. "About Judas you write. Jesus knows he is enemy, but still He washes the feet."

"Oh, that," Nelson said, his expression one of relief. "That thought was from one of our pastor's sermons at church. He was preaching on forgiveness, on how the Lord ministered even to His worst enemies. How He knew the heart of man, yet loved mankind in spite of it. He was always ready to forgive."

Mary slowly shook her head. "I do not know about this forgiving of the enemies. Sometimes that is a very hard thing."

❧

While the setting sun turned Mary's hair to spun gold around her lovely face, Nelson watched an array of emotions play over her exquisite features. His heart went out to her. He could not imagine someone so fragile in appearance having to deal with enemies as vile as the Nazis. If anyone had deserved to be spared from the horrible things that had befallen her country, Mary had. There was something incredibly special about her. And whatever it was, it convinced him that if he had known her before the war, he would have gladly protected her—even single-handedly—from the entire German army.

Of course, before those events occurred, he had been able-bodied. Strong. Whole.

And it wasn't true that he thought of her like a sister. Quite the opposite. But he couldn't allow himself to entertain foolish notions of a more personal nature. One rejection was more than enough to get past. He swallowed a lump in his throat. *Dear Lord, help me to find the right words. Speak through me to help this searching soul.*

"You're right, my friend," he told her. "It is hard to forgive people who've wronged us or caused us harm. It goes against our nature. I felt exactly that same way when I fell on the battlefield. In fact, until the last week or so, I doubted I would ever find a shred of forgiveness inside for anyone I felt was responsible for maiming me."

"But now?" she asked. "You can forgive?"

The depth of pain in her blue green eyes was almost more than Nelson could bear. Her entire family, dead. Such awful suffering had been forced upon this angel-woman. "Yes," he said gently. "But only because the Lord gave me the strength I needed. I couldn't have done it otherwise."

A sad smile softened her lips, and her eyes took on a faraway look. "Those words someone else said. We forgive because God forgives." A ragged breath came from deep inside. "Still, is a hard thing."

Without even thinking about it, Nelson reached over with his free arm and hugged her. "I know, Mary Theresa. I know."

☙

In reflex, Mary almost stiffened and shrugged out of Nelson's embrace, even though she knew it was only a gesture of comfort. But then, she remembered. He considered her just another *sister*. He had no designs on her. She had nothing to fear from him.

As quickly as it occurred, the hug ended.

She tried not to assign to his action any more importance than it deserved. Drawing on one of the most valuable talents she'd acquired at Ravensbruck, she kept her expression passive and did not display any emotion whatsoever.

"Was there anything else you were wondering about?" he asked, as though nothing had happened.

"Small things."

"Well, if you'd like to spell them out, I'll do my best to explain them."

Noticing they were approaching the house, Mary just smiled. "Next time, maybe."

"You got it." His expression took on a sudden brightness. "Say, if you're free on Sunday, you might consider coming to church with us. Our pastor is wonderful in explaining spiritual matters, and he lays things out so simply, even a blockhead like me can understand them."

She met his gaze. "Maybe. Some Sunday."

"Great. Hey, we made it back already." Nelson turned onto the walk leading to the front steps.

Mary put on her best smile and followed, preceding him inside when he paused to open the screen door for her.

"Oh, you're back, you two," Estelle remarked from the dining room. She came toward them, several pieces of silverware still in her hands as she peered outside. "Are we in for a storm? I've been watching the sky."

Mary had completely forgotten the clouds they'd mentioned earlier.

"Wouldn't be surprised," Nelson said. "The radio announcer said a squall might be headed this way."

Wondering if it could possibly compare to the one raging

inside her, Mary affected her original cheerfulness and turned to Estelle. "Needing help?"

"Sure. Extra hands are always welcome here."

ୡ

The ticking of the bedside clock was barely audible against the pounding rain. Feeling utterly worn out, Mary Theresa made no attempt to read her Bible into the late hours. She lay curled up beneath all the blankets she possessed, summer or not, trying to dispel the chill inside her as she mulled over her visit to the Thomases, the more-than-pleasant walk with Nelson.

You have no right to feel slighted, she lectured herself. *You forget you must not think about Estelle's brother.*

"But he is so nice to think about," came her reply in the stillness.

He is a good man. Not like the others. A man of pure thoughts. Too pure for you.

There was no argument against the truth. Clenching her teeth, Mary turned over, covers and all, and expelled a weary sigh.

The aggravating jangle of the alarm clock jolted her awake. Astonished that she'd dozed at all, Mary wondered how in the world she would get through this day. She got up and washed with cold water to help revive herself, then grabbed the first dress she touched and put it on.

Shortly thereafter, when she arrived at the factory, she took comfort from knowing Estelle would be there. She headed straight for the machine.

Mary's spirit took a nosedive. Mrs. Hardwick stood waiting for her. What on earth could she want? "Good morning," she ventured, wishing Estelle had come early. But her friend's machine still wore its muslin cover.

"Malinowski." No actual smile ever made an appearance on the supervisor's mouth. In fact, Mary decided, the only variance in the woman's demeanor occurred when it revealed anger rather than irritation. "You'll be moving to an electric machine today. One of the girls quit yesterday."

"I will? I–I mean. . .yes, Madam." A better machine. Faster work. That meant more pay.

It also meant a different location.

Any elation she might have felt vanished like hoarfrost in the hot sun.

"Come along. We'll get you set up."

Clutching her purse to her chest, Mary trudged behind the surly matron, counting machines as they went. One, two, three. . . How far from Estelle was she going to end up? Fifteen, sixteen. . .

Eventually Mary quit counting.

When Mrs. Hardwick finally halted their march, Mary looked back across the cavernous room. The new—or rather, better—machine couldn't have been farther from her old location unless it had been in an entirely different building.

"Those are your supplies," the woman announced, gesturing toward a metal rack lining the end wall. "You'll find your new quota posted on the machine." With something akin to a smirk, she turned on her heel and strode away.

Mary hugged herself as she took a deep breath and slowly let it out. Olympic Sewing Factory suddenly reminded her a whole lot of a forced labor camp.

eleven

Just finishing up another shirt collar when the noon bell rang, Mary added the article to the others in her basket, then turned off her machine. She snatched her lunch bag and thermos from the bottom drawer and made a beeline for Estelle, approaching her friend from behind. Mischievously, Mary leaned over to peek into the brunette's face.

"There you are!" A look of profound relief subtracted frown lines from Estelle's perpetually cheerful expression. "I've been getting a stiff neck all morning trying to find you."

Smiling, Mary cast a wistful look at her old machine, still bearing stacks of unfinished sleeve parts, as if waiting for her to sit down and get to work. Perhaps it was being serviced and oiled for its next attendant. "A nice day, it is. Outside we eat?"

"Sure. Just let me grab my stuff."

Not wanting to waste any of the limited time available, they hurriedly exited the factory. Along the exterior of the drab, tan building, other Olympic workers stretched their legs and chatted. A few smoked cigarettes. Mary and Estelle filled their lungs with the fresh ocean breeze, appreciating even a short respite from the stuffy confines of the workplace as they made their way toward a shaded bench half a block's distance away.

"Where on earth did you end up?" Estelle asked on their walk. "When I arrived at my machine and saw a stranger occupying yours, I felt like I'd lost my only friend."

"My machine? A new girl there is?" After all the effort Mary had put forth to meet her quota on the old relic, she'd nevertheless harbored a slim hope that her move would prove temporary. And the fact that no one had been occupying it when she reached Estelle gave the impression that it was vacant. Now she knew she must accept the grim reality of permanence.

"Yes," Estelle moaned as they took seats. "Gertrude something or other. She's nice enough and all, but the girl is all thumbs, and that's no exaggeration. Maybe it's from trying too hard or something, but so far, she's managed to break two needles, chip a tip off her scissors, and she has yet to do a single sleeve properly."

Remembering how awkward she'd felt on her own first day, Mary couldn't help chuckling.

Estelle rolled her eyes. "Old Lady Hardwick's been breathing down our necks all morning, barking orders. Needless to say, I didn't want to risk drawing even more attention by asking after your whereabouts." She reached into her lunch sack and took out an apple.

"Poor you." Mary Theresa sympathized as she unwrapped a ham and cheese sandwich and began eating.

As always, Estelle bowed her head for a brief prayer before biting into the crisp fruit. "Poor me!" she exclaimed afterward. "What about you? Where'd she stick you?"

"Other end of world," Mary quipped wryly. "Against back wall. Too much we were liking work together, I think."

"No doubt." Estelle's light laugh somehow lacked mirth. "Well, at least on sunny days we can come here and have a short visit. Have you made a friend at your new station?" She crunched into her apple, a teasing gleam in her eye. "It probably won't take much to replace me, sad to say."

A sheepish grin broke across Mary's lips. "English I pretend not understanding. What good is to make friend, if just to split up?"

At that, Estelle smiled and shook her head. "You're right." Then she sighed. "Lunch is the only time we'll have now. And

I'd really started enjoying our snatches of conversation each new day. It made coming to work much more pleasurable."

"For me, too." The hot tea which usually perked Mary up during the break now only made her sleepy. Considering her restlessness throughout the previous night, she knew it would be a struggle to stay awake until quitting time. She poured out the contents of the thermos cup and recapped the bottle, then brushed the crumbs from her lap onto the sidewalk for the pigeons cooing about them. So much leisure time the birds had, strutting about in the mild, clean air.

"Well, you'll still be coming to supper on Tuesday nights. Okay?" Estelle asked a little too brightly. "At least we'll have something to look forward to in this new, otherwise colorless existence."

Mary feigned a smile, her best attempt to match her friend's levity. "Maybe. Sure."

Mutually disappointed at this new turn of events, they lapsed into a short span of silence, watching the passing traffic as they ate.

Suddenly Estelle stopped chewing. "Hey! I have an idea!"

"What is it?"

"On the other hand," she said tentatively, "I guess it depends on whether you already go to church somewhere on Sundays. Does your host family come to get you every week?"

"No. Other direction is Saint Hedwig's. Not to bother, I tell them. Other churches near me." Mary shrugged. "But go, I do not. To walk in alone, sit alone. . ."

Estelle's chocolate eyes focused on her. "Then, it's settled. You're coming with me and my family to church on Sundays. We'll come by and pick you up. Afterward, you can have dinner with us. It'll help make up for being separated at work. What do you think?"

Mary hesitated. "More bother I would be."

"Are you kidding?" With a look of disbelief, Estelle leaned

closer and hugged her. "You couldn't be a bother if you tried. But—" She sobered. "If you think you'd feel uncomfortable attending worship with us, don't think you have to come just to please me. I'll understand."

"New to me is this Protestant church," Mary admitted. "How to know if I like or not like?"

"You mean, you'll actually give it a try?"

At the hope in her friend's dark eyes, Mary didn't have the heart to refuse. *Besides,* she told herself, perhaps it *won't be so very different from what I am used to.* After all, they did worship the same God. And what could it hurt, to spend an extra day with these dear people who made her feel so at home? Or to be around Nelson. . .

❧

"This must be it," Nelson heard his father say as he steered into an empty space along the right curb. He applied the hand brake, then turned off the engine.

"Right, Daddy. I'll go get Mary." Seated behind their father, Estelle opened her door and jumped out. In a matter of seconds, she disappeared into the broad foyer of a squat two-story building whose ground floor housed a watch repair shop on one side and a millinery on the other. Above were a number of apartments.

Since his door was on the passenger side, Nelson also got out to wait by the car. No sense making Mary Theresa walk around the entire vehicle to get in. He slid one hand into the pocket of his dress slacks and idly assessed the neighborhood, noting other neatly kept establishments interspersed by occasional large dwellings. Fair-sized maples and box elder trees provided mottled shade to the sidewalks lining the street.

Detecting the approaching chatter and giggles that invariably preceded his bubbly sister, he turned to see her emerge and start down the steps. The squirt looked particularly appealing with her dark waves gleaming against the vibrant cranberry red dress Mom had finished a few days before. Her white hat and high heels accented the tiny polka dots and white trim, enhancing her shapely legs. *Not bad,* Nelson decided, *even for a sister.*

But when Mary Theresa stepped into view, a ray of sunshine lit upon the fairest rose in all the kingdom. In a filmy long-sleeved dress of delicate pink, she needed no adornment but the strand of pearls gracing her neck. Beneath a small, straw-colored hat, and freed from the normal confinement of rolls and pins, her side-parted hair fell to her shoulders in a soft honey-gold pageboy. A pearl barrette rested behind one ear.

Nelson had to remind himself to close his mouth.

Maybe this wasn't such a great idea, taking her to church. . . where any guy with eyes in his head was certain to snap her up.

The loveliest of smiles parted her lips as she and Stella approached. "Good morning, everybody," she said, oblivious to the glorious vision she made.

"Morning," they all chorused.

Nelson gave himself a mental shake, then cleared his throat. "Hope you don't mind the middle." He moved aside to allow Mary enough room to climb in while Stella went around to her seat.

"Is fine," she said softly, lifting her lashes to meet his gaze. Pausing, she handed him her Bible to hold, then turned, and lowered herself to the seat. "Oh!" she gasped, as the narrow ruffle at her wrist snagged on his watch.

"No problem." Nelson freed the errant thread almost as quickly as it had caught.

But not quickly enough to prevent that glimpse of her delicate forearm.

Or the numbers tattooed in black.

Feeling as if he'd just taken a punch to the stomach, Nelson climbed in beside Mary. A barrage of questions, like the rat-tat-tat of an enemy machine gun, shot through his mind. What untold horrors had those remarkable eyes witnessed? Had her own family been slaughtered in front of her? And what about her? What kinds of tortures had those inhuman Nazi animals inflicted on this fragile creature, with no one to protect her from harm?

Why hadn't bigmouth Stella made some mention of her friend's background. . .unless Mary had kept the fact that she'd been imprisoned in a concentration camp a secret even from her.

And if so, why?

In any event, a lot of things suddenly made a whole lot of sense.

⁊⁊

"Oh, isn't this just the grandest of days?" Estelle gushed, straightening her skirt as the car pulled out into the light Sunday traffic. Retrieving her slim shoulder bag and Bible from the window ledge behind the seat, she placed them on her lap.

"Yes, simply delightful," her mother replied. She turned to Mary, a gracious smile plumping her cheeks. "We're so happy you could come with us this morning, Dear."

Returning the older woman's smile, Mary Theresa nodded. Her insides quavered as she tried to ignore being crammed a touch too closely to Nelson in the backseat of the family car. She could feel the warmth emanating from him. Or was it her? Had he seen the loathsome brand she'd been so careful to hide from the world? Did he know her shame?

She doubted she could bear knowing if he'd discovered her dreaded secret, yet the possibility of not knowing seemed somehow even less bearable. Hesitantly, she raised a timid gaze in his direction.

Nelson seemed absorbed in the passing scenery. But as if sensing her attention, he turned to her, the typically friendly smile on his lips and in his eyes.

His face revealed nothing!

Mary dared to relax. Somewhat.

"Oh, look, Mom," Estelle said. "They've painted that charming little shop we like so much. And added shutters. Doesn't it look absolutely divine?"

Mary tuned out the exchange between mother and daughter and concentrated instead on how incredibly dashing her friend's brother looked in the navy serge suit he wore. The tie knotted at his throat had flecks of the same light brown as his eyes, and his shiny mahogany hair had been neatly slicked back. All that walking in the sunshine had added an appealing light bronze cast to his clear complexion, only increasing his appeal.

Mary barely suppressed an unbidden sigh.

If circumstances had only been different, had she been born in America instead of Poland, perhaps she could have been Nelson's girl.

What are you thinking? she berated herself. *You are here to attend church with this family. For you, that is more than you should have expected.*

"Well," Mr. Thomas announced in his usual pleasant way, "we're here. He turned the car onto a street running alongside the church and parked in the first available spot.

The men got out first. Nelson gave no indication it had been a struggle. He'd certainly made remarkable progress since the last time Mary had seen him. He opened his mother's door, offered a hand to her, and then to Mary.

Placing her cool fingers into his much warmer ones, Mary again chanced a look at him. Surely he must have caught a glimpse of the wretched tattoo. How could he not? It practically shouted out her shame. He had to know.

But if he did, he gave no sign of it.

twelve

This small, but tidy, place of worship seemed nowhere near the size of the churches which Mary Theresa had visited during her lifetime. But she found the pristine white steeple crowning the red brick structure quite charming, with its plain metal cross gilded by sunlight against the cloudless sky. She sensed a cordial welcome among the other arrivals greeting one another with smiles and handclasps. Nevertheless, a tiny niggle of unfamiliarity fluttered inside her like a flock of butterflies, and she wondered what to expect.

The bell in the tower pealed as the family headed for the steps leading to the main entrance. "Late again," moaned Estelle as she picked up the pace.

Once inside, Mary caught only the briefest glimpse of the sanctuary upon entering the foyer. Estelle grabbed a hand and drew her to a downward staircase, with Nelson following cautiously behind. Mr. and Mrs. Thomas headed in an entirely different direction. "We have Sunday school before the main service," Estelle explained, "with other people in our age group."

Somewhat winded after mounting the outside staircase and then descending this one, it took Mary a moment to catch her breath as they paused outside a closed door, waiting for Nelson.

With a scarcely noticeable limp, he caught up and opened it for them, and the threesome stepped inside a carpeted room whose plain walls held only a blackboard, a calendar with a painting of Christ, and a few colored pictures of Bible scenes in matching wood frames. A bulletin board near the door sported a mishmash of notices and pictures of missionaries thumbtacked to its cork surface.

Two dozen strange faces peered up from the circle of folding chairs ringing the room.

Unpleasant experiences from the death camp, of times when too much attention was centered on her and a few fellow prisoners, assaulted Mary's mind. She felt vulnerable and exposed, and unconsciously she shrank backward. Into Nelson.

"They don't bite," he whispered, giving her shoulder a reassuring squeeze.

Drawing on that encouragement, Mary followed Estelle to three empty chairs. With her friend seated on one side and Nelson on the other, she felt a little of the tension inside her abate. Now if only everyone would stop staring. . .

A young man with freckles and a crew cut, obviously the leader, spoke first. "Hi, Stell, Nelson, and. . .?"

"My friend, Mary Theresa Malinowski," Estelle supplied.

"Glad to have you with us, Mary," he grinned, initiating smiles and interest from the others. "I'm Lennie Richards. I'll let the rest of this mob introduce themselves at the close. To catch you late-birds up, our study of the Gospel of John brings us to the account of the condemned woman, in chapter eight, if you'd like to turn there."

Estelle and Nelson found the passage quickly, but Mary had to resort to checking her Bible's table of contents first, all the while detecting more than a little scrutiny from some of the young men in the group. Finally reaching the specified chapter, she swallowed and tucked her pinpricked fingers beneath her Bible, wishing she'd at least remembered her lace gloves.

Lennie leaned forward, an open Bible in one hand as he took up where he'd apparently left off before their arrival. "Remember, there was no question about guilt here. None whatsoever. The case was cut-and-dried. The gal had been caught in the act of adultery and brought before Jesus. There she stood, in the middle of the crowd He'd been teaching, all eyes upon her. Now the question was, what punishment should she receive?"

Completely relating to the victim in the story, Mary wanted to crawl into a hole and die.

"Wait, wait, wait," Estelle cut in, raising her arm to halt the proceedings. She wagged her head. "And where was the man, I ask you? Honestly. Since way back in the Garden of Eden, we women have had to take the blame for everything. Did Eve hear God state the rules of the place? No. She got it all secondhand, from old Adam. It was all hearsay."

The other young ladies present stifled giggles behind their hands as they exchanged surreptitious glances between themselves. They seemed more than willing to allow her to be their voice.

"Yeah," a gap-toothed fellow with prominent ears piped up. "But even so, she embellished it, didn't she? Women always have to tack something on to a story, make it a little juicier, and it started at the beginning of time. Things haven't changed much, either."

A collective snicker of agreement came from the male segment.

"Humph." Estelle crossed her arms. "Well, I have to admit, something has always bothered me about certain passages. How do you justify that all through the Old Testament, kings and patriarchs thought nothing at all of wedding a few dozen wives and taking a multitude of concubines on the side?" Her voice raised momentarily. "What's fair about that? It's the old double standard, plain and simple."

"I agree," a fair-faced redhead with blond eyebrows said, a rosy glow advertising her reticence to speak out, especially on such a sensitive subject. "Why must women always take the blame, and never the men?"

" 'Cause that's the way it's supposed to be," said one of
the guys who'd been less than discreet in his bold appraisal
of Mary.

Quite aware of that fresh perusal as she listened to a few
more arguments along that line being bandied about, Mary
felt a warm flush of her own, as if she were the woman
standing before that judgmental mob. What if Nelson truly
had seen her tattoo, guessed what she had done? She clasped
her hands in her lap, wishing she could get up and walk out,
find someplace to hide.

As if picking up on her discomfiture, Nelson finally stepped
into the fray, his voice firm, yet gentle. "I think we're all getting offtrack here, people. The whole point of the passage is
not guilt or punishment, per se. The Pharisees were attempting
to trip Jesus up in the matter of Jewish law. The fact is, in
God's perfect plan, He advocated one man and one woman, in
marriage for life. And in Israel's covenant, the law dictated
death to both parties in almost all cases of adultery. But Rome
had taken away the right of the Jews to inflict the death
penalty, which in this case happened to be by stoning. They
were hoping to trap Jesus between His allegiance to the law—
which ran counter to Rome's decrees—and His mercy and
love toward even those who violated it—which would lower
the moral standard. Either way He decided, they figured they
had Him."

"Amen," Lennie breathed, relief written all over his freckles. "Say on, Nelse."

"But, as always, Jesus knew the hearts of those dignitaries,"
Nelson continued. "And He knew the one thing that would trip
them up. Which is why He suggested that whichever one of
them who was without sin should cast the first stone. Can't
you picture all those proud teachers of men, their faces turning
red, slinking quietly away?"

Heads nodded in agreement around the circle.

"Even today, we must consider our own faults and failures before we jump onto someone else's. All of us have something in our lives to be ashamed of. Let's not be so quick to condemn others."

Just then the bell in the tower signaled the call to worship.

"Well said, Nelson," Lennie declared with an emphatic nod and clapped his Bible shut. "We're sure glad to have you back. Now let's close in prayer."

Mary Theresa let out a slow breath. The class had finally ended. Her heart swelled with gratitude over the way Nelson had come to her rescue like an undeclared champion.

Then the other shoe fell. For him to have defended her, he must have seen the tattoo.

≈∙

After the morning worship service, as their little group headed homeward, Nelson let the other members of his family compare their impressions of the finer points of the pastor's sermon without any input from him. He had other things on his mind. Conscious of Mary Theresa's presence beside him, his ears perked up a little whenever she spoke, but the rest of the time he tuned everything out.

He felt rather pleased with his performance in Sunday school. He hadn't intended to take over the discussion and, in fact, had planned to sit back as he had done last week and listen to those younger guys talk. But when it became apparent that the class had gotten out of hand and that Mary Theresa was in distress, a need to protect her rose to the fore.

And she'd had every reason to be uncomfortable, Nelson concluded bitterly, the way Barry Sanders had stared at her. And Rob Denton hadn't been very subtle in the way he'd ogled her, either, considering the young man was supposedly going steady with Pastor Herman's granddaughter, Melody.

Of course, Nelson reminded himself, both those guys had

excellent jobs. Promising futures. When it came right down to it, they had a whole lot more to offer someone like Mary than he did.

Whoa! What was he thinking? His own former true love had dumped him the instant she learned about the loss of his lower leg. What made him think someone perfect—much less rare and exquisite, like Mary—would give serious consideration to a guy who'd been maimed, and who spent most of his time sitting on his backside, letting the savings from his allotment checks rot in the bank?

Fact was, he felt a whole lot better about himself now that he'd tossed the crutches and started using his artificial leg. It seemed incredible how much more relaxed people were around him, how they treated him the same way they had before the war. Maybe it was time to consider going to work again. At least do that much.

"What did you think about that, Nelson?" Dad was saying.

"Hmm? Oh. Sorry, I wasn't listening. My mind was elsewhere."

"Asleep, more than likely," Estelle chided. "After using up a year's supply of brainpower in Sunday school."

"How's that?" his mother asked.

"Just the usual male versus female thing," she answered. "No sooner do I get to put in my two cents then Nelson charges forward like a knight ready to do battle. Nobody got a word in edgewise after that."

"Probably scared little Mary to death, with such goings-on," Mom said.

"Oh, I don't know," Estelle returned. "She was really quite a hit. The guys were all admiring her. A couple of them in particular."

"Do not say such things," Mary said quietly, her head lowering.

Picturing that bunch of young guys leering at Mary Theresa,

like wolves circling helpless prey, Nelson ground his teeth. He looked up at his father. "Say, Dad, I've been wondering. Suppose Mr. Gavin's still holding my old job open, the way he promised? Think I might try going back to work."

"Well, that is good news," his father said, meeting his gaze in the rearview mirror.

"An answer to prayer," Mom added. "A real answer to prayer. We'll have to celebrate." She turned around to Mary. "I do hope you still have an appetite, Dear. You will be coming to dinner, of course, won't you?"

"A. . .headache I have," Mary said, with that trapped look about her. "I should go home."

Nelson's spirit flagged. She had to know he'd monopolized Sunday school for her benefit and hers alone. Or was it just him she wanted to avoid? Thank heaven he hadn't humiliated himself by asking her out. One small blessing he could be grateful for.

"Oh, nonsense," Mom countered. "That's nothing a little bit of aspirin won't cure. We have plenty of that at home. We'll get you fixed up right and proper. See if we don't."

♨

Mary knew exactly how a mouse felt when the trap snapped on its tail. She hadn't exactly disliked her foray into the different style of worship. Granted, that plain sanctuary with its simple wooden cross backlit behind the pulpit could have used some sprucing up. A few statues, some embroidered cloths on the altar, a bank of flickering candles. . . But all in all, she'd liked the hymns with their lovely music and words, and the soloist had performed flawlessly, as well. And the pastor's sermon, in English rather than Latin, had stirred her heart, taking her back to those Bible readings she'd found so comforting in the barracks.

And even that class—what did they call it—Sunday school. Especially Nelson's standing up for her. Even now she felt his very real presence next to her on the seat. She tried to shift a little closer to Estelle.

Except for the topic which had hit a bit close to home, her thoughts rambled on, *it was quite an experience to hear young people discussing religion and its practical application to one's life.* She'd never had much interest in such things in her younger years. Her parents and siblings attended Mass only sporadically, and none of them seemed to feel a lack.

Not until Ravensbruck did Mary begin to grasp how very deeply Almighty God loved mankind, how precious and real His presence seemed to those who trusted Him with their very lives. Even in that hellish place, amid the indescribable suffering, His peace was available to anyone who reached out for it. Where one worshipped God wasn't the most important thing. It was a matter of the heart that counted.

But still, all of that happened in the past. What about the present problem? Now that she'd gone to church with her friend's family, even enjoyed some portions of it, she wanted to go home. Be by herself. Ponder everything she'd heard.

And that was the one thing she couldn't do. In misery, she looked out the corner of her eye at Nelson. . .who strangely didn't appear any more thrilled about her coming than she was.

Of course, he'd had more time to think about that hateful brand. He'd surely guessed her shame. Perhaps he knew. . . everything.

thirteen

Nelson brought up the rear of the oddly quiet group as his family and Mary Theresa trailed into the house after church.

"I'll change and get dinner going," his mom announced, heading for the stairs. Already tugging his tie loose, Dad clomped after her.

"Come on, Mare," Estelle said. "Soon as I put on a more comfortable dress, I'll go find you some aspirin for your headache."

Nelson slipped off his suit jacket and watched in sullen silence as the two girls started up the steps. When he heard his sister's bedroom door close, he ascended to his own room at a slower pace.

No wonder Mary Theresa had a headache, he told himself, after so much attention was drawn to her at Sunday School, then sitting through a long worship service that probably seemed strange and foreign to her. And of course, Stella invariably talked the girl's ears off all the time. But then, why should he complain about that? It kept him from having to make so much conversation himself.

Changing into casual slacks and a short-sleeved cotton shirt, he continued mulling over the day's happenings.

By the time he came back downstairs, he discovered that the others had already beaten him. He crossed to his chair, bent to pick up the Sunday paper on the floor beside it, then took a seat.

Stella's impatient voice drifted from the kitchen. "That's what I've been trying to tell you. It's all gone. Really. The bottle's in the medicine cabinet, but it's empty. I looked for another one, but there wasn't any."

"How odd. I know we just bought that a few weeks ago," Mom replied, her voice somewhat muffled by the door she closed whenever she had the oven going. "Maybe Nelson's been taking it to ease the pain of walking with that wooden leg. I know it bothered him quite a lot at first. You'll just have to run to Murphy's and get more. I believe this is his Sunday to be open for emergencies."

"Oh, Mom. . ." Stella groused. "It's hot out. Are you sure there's no other aspirin in the house? Maybe in your purse?"

"No, Dear, that was all we had."

"Is no problem," Mary Theresa said. "Only small headache I have. Fine I am."

But Nelson doubted his mom would allow anything to dissuade her from that inborn compulsion to mother their guest. She reveled in it. He almost smiled when he heard her reply.

"Small headache or not, I'm sure you're very uncomfortable. The drugstore is just down at the corner. It'll only take Stella a few minutes. She'll be back in no time."

"Then I, too, go," Mary Theresa offered. "I'll keep her company."

"In that bright sun? I won't hear of it." The kitchen faucet ran momentarily, then ceased. "Now, I've wrung out a nice cool cloth for your head. You just come sit down in the parlor and close your eyes. Put your feet up. We'll have you better in no time." The kitchen door opened, and three sets of footsteps came down the hallway.

While Stella took her leave, Nelson watched a white-faced Mary being guided into the front room, right past him, to his father's favorite overstuffed chair near the fireplace. "Here," Mom insisted, gently pushing her down onto the seat cushion. "Lay your head back. Yes, like that. And put this washcloth on your forehead. Here's the hassock to rest your feet. And you won't need these high heels on, either." One by one, she slipped Mary's shoes off, then placed them together on the floor, within easy reach.

The whole scene would have been comical, Nelson supposed, if he hadn't been in such a mood. Stella pouting her way out the door, Mary Theresa approaching the parlor as if to face a firing squad, Mom so absorbed in the chance to fuss over somebody, she was completely oblivious to all else. That left only Dad out of things. Where was he, anyway?

Just then, the older man's heavy footfalls echoed along the upstairs hall and down the risers. Nelson's eyes widened. Instead of the typical Sunday afternoon attire his father wore in case relatives dropped by unexpectedly, he had on his grubby chore clothes. "Thought I'd change the oil in the car," he said, meeting Nelson's gaze. "It seemed to idle a little rough this morning; did you notice?"

"Who, me? No."

"Well, no sense waiting till old Jenny gives out on us altogether, when there's plenty of time today to set her to perking again." With a conspiratorial wink at Mom, he sauntered toward the rear of the house.

"Guess I'll see about dinner," she said with a little shrug, and traipsed up the hall again.

The back door closed with a click. The kitchen door whooshed shut.

And the loudest silence Nelson had ever experienced settled over the front room.

Across from him, with her forehead and eyes shrouded beneath a worn, pink washcloth, Mary Theresa sat so still she scarcely appeared to be breathing.

The mantel clock ticked, ticked, ticked.

Nelson gave a silent huff. "Nice day today, wasn't it? Always did like midsummer in New York."

Mary Theresa moistened her lips.

A few more minutes passed.

So that's how it was gonna be, was it? Well, he wasn't about to take on sole responsibility of entertaining the troops. That was the USO's job. Picking up another section of the Sunday paper, he snapped it open.

"You saw, didn't you?" she finally asked.

"Excuse me?" Having a fairly clear idea what Mary meant, Nelson didn't have the heart to come clean, not after all the trouble she'd gone through to keep that tattoo hidden from the world. Always wearing long sleeves, no matter how hot the weather. Protecting her from the truth would be easy enough. After all, it was the gallant thing to do, and all.

Then again, perhaps he'd misread her. Maybe she meant something else entirely. That was marginally possible, wasn't it?

She raised a corner of the cloth, peeking at him through one eye.

"Oh. You mean, the way all the guys at class were gawking at you?" he hedged. "They weren't exactly subtle about it, you know."

Mary hesitated for an instant, then lifted her head, and the washcloth dropped to her lap. She toyed with it as she focused on Nelson. "Uncomfortable it makes me, to have people looking at me. I do not like."

"Well, you might as well face it, Mary Theresa," he said with a half-smile, "the Lord didn't exactly cut corners when He made you. I don't know when I've ever come across a more beautiful woman in my life."

Expecting her to warm to the compliment and perhaps even blush a little, Nelson watched her expression deflate instead. Incredibly, the edges of her lips wilted sadly.

"A curse it is," she disclosed. "Too much it draws attention."

How was a guy supposed to respond to that? All the women he knew seemed to want a man to notice them, to appreciate the effort they'd put into looking attractive and appealing. Otherwise, there'd be a lot less in the way of coy looks and short skirts around, wouldn't there?

Mary Theresa expelled a tired breath. Tipping her head back once more, she closed her eyes and replaced the pink blindfold.

Watching her withdraw into that private shell, Nelson allowed himself a leisurely evaluation of her glistening hair, slim curves, tiny feet. . .and for the life of him, could see nothing remotely resembling a curse. Yet she wore shyness like a feather quilt about herself. What could possibly have happened during the war to make her feel she had to keep hiding?

He'd seen newsreels of the pathetic souls who'd been confined behind all that barbed wire, their emaciated forms, hollow eyes, hopeless faces, shaved heads. He glanced at Mary's crowning glory, wondering if she'd been made to suffer that humiliation. But in any event, at least she came out of the camp alive. *That must count for something,* he reasoned.

But then his more sympathetic side took over. From the few things Mary had told him and the family, Nelson knew she had no living relatives. That had to hurt more than anything else. And, judging from her age and the years Poland was involved in its struggle to survive, she'd likely missed out on a goodly chunk of her education, which could account for her lack of confidence in herself. And as far as resources, he had no clue about how she'd managed immigrating to America or what her financial situation might be now. He did know that job at the sewing factory didn't pay much—he'd seen Stella's paychecks. Maybe all those things, plus her limited proficiency in English, made her feel inadequate.

But why would she feel that way here, of all places, among people who truly. . .cared? Because, he might as well accept it, he already cared about Mary Theresa more than he'd ever intended. And that was the problem.

By the time the screen door squeaked open, and his frazzled

sister came in, the distinctive aroma of fried chicken floated deliciously through the house. She held a paper sack high in triumph. "Success at last!"

Mary Theresa sat up.

"Sure took you long enough," Nelson mused.

Brushing a sheen of perspiration from her forehead with her fingertips, Stella arched her eyebrows. "Well, I ended up having to go all the way to Jenkins's Drugstore. Murphy's wasn't open today after all."

"Oh. So sorry I am for the trouble," Mary crooned.

"It wasn't any bother, really. Only another couple blocks. The breeze kept me cool, and part of the walk was shady. The important thing is we can now take care of that headache. Come on. Time's a wasting. Mmm. Dinner smells good. I'm starving."

Nelson couldn't help noting how quickly Mary Theresa made her escape.

Nor did he miss the wary glance she flicked in his direction as she went by.

Oh, well, he decided. A lot of serious stuff was going on in that pretty head of hers. Some other time maybe he'd probe a little more, next time he had her alone. Find out what all she was hiding.

ю.

Later that evening, soaking in a hot bath, Mary relived that unbelievably long day. She'd rather enjoyed the church service, if not the Sunday school class—and she might have liked even that, had the topic been something a little less personal. It seemed no matter where she turned, her past was thrown in her face. Was there no escape from it, ever?

Yet, as her thoughts drifted back to the Reverend Herman's message, she found herself drawing on its comfort. She'd never thought about Jesus' crucifixion as being God's plan from before the dawning of time. But, the pastor explained, only a perfect, innocent sacrifice would satisfy a holy God and cover the sin of mankind. For that purpose, He gave up His own Son to come to earth as a babe and to die that awful death on the cross. Mary's heart swelled at the thought of such immeasurable love.

But then again, her conscience taunted, *there were sins, and then there were* sins. Maybe some offenses were too vile to be forgiven. And she suspected hers might be among those.

On that bleak thought, Mary stepped out of the tub to towel off. Then in her blue flannel robe, she padded out to her sofa and sat hugging her knees to her breast.

Today had been a close call. Too close. She didn't relish putting herself in that kind of situation ever again. Maybe Nelson knew about her identification number, and maybe he didn't. If he did, Mary could only hope he'd keep her secret from his family. After all, what purpose would it serve for the horrible truth to become common knowledge?

But even if he didn't know about it, there was every possibility that somehow, someday he'd discover it anyway. . . unless she stopped going to the Thomas home entirely.

That wrenching thought filled her with a loneliness as deep as the one she'd felt when she and Rahel had kissed one another's cheeks and embraced in final farewell in Switzerland. Neither of them could bring themselves to speak aloud, but to her dying day she would hear her Jewish friend's whisper. *Kocham Ciebie. Do widzenia. . .I love you. Good-bye.*

Could she bear to give up these special times with this precious new American friend who'd become as close as a sister? Be satisfied only to chat with Estelle at lunchtime and let it go at that? Never to see the parents who had made her feel as special as a daughter? Or the brother, Nelson. . .whose own wounded soul had somehow reached out to hers from the moment they met?

With a shuddering sigh, Mary Theresa knew it was time to

give that unthinkable resolution some serious consideration.

A heavy weight descended upon her spirit. Hoping to find strength and solace, she picked up the Bible that Nelson had given her and opened it at random. But her blood turned cold. Instead of the peace she so sorely wanted, her eyes focused on the admonition from the fifth chapter of James: *Confess your faults one to another. . . .*

fourteen

Bright and early the next morning, Nelson followed the tantalizing smell of bacon down to its source.

"Morning," Stella said, passing him on her way to the door.

"Squirt," he returned good-naturedly. "Work up a storm."

She wrinkled her nose at him. "I liked going to work a whole lot better when we were making army uniforms. It seemed so much more important, back then." Snagging her purse and lunch bag from the hall tree, she left.

Nelson watched after his sister for several seconds, appreciating the way she looked in her violet jumper and print blouse. She had tamed her curls a bit with the addition of a twisted scarf, tied ribbon style, with the ends dangling behind one ear. *Jonathan could do a lot worse,* he decided. Stella had taken her fiancé's death at sea pretty hard, but maybe she was finally getting beyond it. Nelson thought he'd detected a few lingering glances in Jon's direction the last time his friend was here. And it was about time. She needed to get on with her life.

And Sis wasn't the only one. He'd be hiking to the trolley himself, shortly, then catching the subway across town to talk to his former boss and see about getting his old job back. If that worked out, perhaps in time he could start giving some thought to getting married and settling down. Other guys like him had found girls willing to look beyond their handicaps.

And children. He'd like that. Thoughts of Mary Theresa flew into his mind and so did the admiration she'd gotten from the other guys at church. When a woman was as perfect as she and could have her pick of men, why would she consider him?

Filling his lungs and exhaling slowly, Nelson continued on to the kitchen, where he could hear his parents' voices as he approached and entered.

"Hi, Mom. Hi, Dad."

"Morning, Son. You're looking chipper today."

"Yes, isn't he?" At the stove, his mother smiled. "Good morning, Dear." She broke two more eggs into the frying pan to sizzle, then put bread into the toaster. "Breakfast will be right on."

Nelson caught a mysterious glance pass between his parents as he took his usual spot at the kitchen table, but didn't think much about it until his dad tacked on a sly wink. That added to the definite undercurrent Nelson sensed in the room. He cleared his throat. "I decided today was as good a day as any to go see Mr. Gavin about my old job. In a little while, I'll go hop on the trolley."

The older pair just grinned.

Tucking his chin in puzzlement, Nelson threw his hands up. "Okay, I give. What's going on?" He looked from one of them to the other.

"What do you mean?" his father asked in all innocence.

Mom brought over the plate of food and set it before Nelson, her smile looking ready to explode from ear to ear any second.

"I know something's up with you two, or you wouldn't look like cats who'd just swallowed canaries. Come on, come clean."

His dad nodded in acquiescence. "Well, no sense letting your breakfast get cold. Eat up. When you're done, your mother and I have a surprise for you."

After bowing his head for a brief prayer of thanks, Nelson dug into his meal. But it was hard to enjoy it with those two waiting with baited breath for him to finish. He finally wolfed it down without tasting any of it, then scorched his throat on two gulps of hot coffee. He wiped his mouth on the napkin.

"Guess it's time," Dad said, getting up and crossing to the back door, Mom only a step behind. "Come with us, Son. We have something to show you."

His parents led him out the kitchen door and down the steps to the alley, where they turned in the direction of MacDougal's Garage on the corner.

Nelson had known barrel-chested Sean MacDougal practically all his life. A redheaded giant with a heart as big as the world, the Scotsman loved to tinker around with cars. He kept almost all the cars in the neighborhood running their best, and never seemed too busy to instruct any lad interested in taking up the trade. When Nelson joined up with the army, Mac generously offered to keep Nelson's car at the garage for him until his return.

The little black coupe had been Nelson's pride and joy. During his time in Europe, he'd often pictured it sitting idle behind MacDougal's, collecting rust and spiderwebs. Not wanting to learn the extent of its deterioration, he'd purposely avoided going to see the man since he'd come home. He had no use for the car, anyway. And now Dad wanted to rub it in?

Nelson held back a little, trying to prepare himself for the moment he would see this sad reminder of his former life. But his parents walked right toward the antiquated garage with its peeling exterior, and opened the wide, wooden door to the shop.

Daylight fell across the interior of the grimy work area cluttered with tires, car parts, and smelling of metal and grease. Everywhere there was an available spot, things were either piled on it, stacked under it, or suspended above on wall hooks.

The Scotsman looked up with a grin, still holding a polishing rag as he finished shining the hood of Nelson's all-too-familiar Chevy. "Nelse, me lad. 'Tis grand to be seein' ye." Wiping his smudged fingers on the rag, he extended an arm.

"Mac." Nelson grabbed the beefy hand and shook it, still not entirely sure what was happening, why his folks had brought him here.

His father patted a fender as he strode around to the driver's side, a smug expression on his face. "Looks pretty good, huh?" He opened the door.

"Sure does," Nelson had to admit. But that only made him feel worse. Surely they realized it was completely useless to him now.

"We rigged her up with a hand clutch, Mac and me," Dad went on. "Thought if you were going back to work, you'd be needing a car."

"A hand clutch?" Had he heard right? Nelson moved around to peer inside, where the sight of the new addition rendered him nearly speechless.

"Your father worked all yesterday afternoon on this," his mother supplied. "He wanted to surprise you."

"I. . .don't know what to say." He should have thought to do that himself. . .and would have, if he hadn't been wallowing in self-pity. Some aspiring engineer he turned out to be.

"We love you," she replied, as if that explained everything.

Blinking away the stinging behind his eyes, he grabbed them both in a big hug, while Mac beamed on from the side, nodding his head. "Well, I love you, too. You guys are the best," Nelson declared, his voice hoarse. "All of you."

"What say we go try her out?" his father suggested.

Nelson itched to do just that. "I'm game. Might take me awhile to get the hang of it, though."

"Take all the time you need, Son. I'm in no hurry. Bill's covering for me at the shop this morning. I called him last night and told him I'd probably be in late."

While his dad went around to the passenger side, Nelson leaned over to give his mom one more hug, then eased himself into the coupe, finding the key already in the ignition. The engine caught on the first try. He cut a glance to his father.

"Mac and I started her up every so often while you were away. We knew you'd need her sooner or later."

Nelson could only shake his head, wondering if he'd ever stop grinning like a sap. They rolled down the windows, his father resting an elbow on the ledge of his. Then with a jaunty wave to Mom and Sean MacDougal, Nelson eased the coupe cautiously out of the shop and into the street, past rows of houses he'd about memorized over the years, past shops he'd frequented since his boyhood, heading for parts unknown.

So quickly it came back, this feeling of normalcy. He grinned at his dad, whose grin mirrored his own. Just wait till Jonathan saw this. And Mary Theresa. . . Somehow it mattered for her to approve. After all, she was largely responsible for his being up and around again. Dare he imagine her occupying the passenger seat, golden hair blowing in the wind, enjoying a drive in the country? He emitted a silent sigh.

Nelson adapted amazingly quickly to the process of applying the clutch by hand to change gears, a feat he could only attribute to his experience of riding friends' motorcycles occasionally during his able-bodied days.

Had it been only a short while ago he'd lain in a hospital bed, certain this part of his life had ended for good, that he'd never experience the freedoms he'd always taken for granted? Now it seemed the Lord planned to give it all back to him, perhaps might have done so before this if Nelson had trusted Him a little sooner. This unexpected and undeserved blessing humbled him greatly.

"Well, what do you think?" his father asked after they'd driven half the length of Manhattan.

"That God gave me the best parents in the world, and I have a lot to be thankful for. I'm gonna make you and Mom proud of me, I promise."

Dad reached over and gave his good knee a squeeze. "We've

always been proud of you, Nelse. We just want you to be happy."

મ

Another cloud drifted across the sky, masking the face of the sun, momentarily shading the bench Mary Theresa and Estelle had come to think of as their own. Mary wondered if it was her imagination that every time she looked up into the blue, she counted more clouds, perhaps indicating another storm.

"You seem quiet today," Estelle commented before biting into her egg salad sandwich.

Mary shrugged a shoulder. "A little tired I am." She broke a few chunks of bread crust and tossed it to the growing number of pigeons who'd discovered they could get handouts if they ventured close enough.

"I don't doubt it. For what's supposed to be a day of rest, yesterday turned out to be quite busy for all of us."

Not particularly wanting to rehash all of that, Mary decided to change the subject. "How is new girl? Gertrude."

Estelle arched her eyebrows, an incredulous expression coming forth. "You won't believe the latest. This morning she managed to sew right through the tip of her finger and fingernail."

"Ouch."

"Yes. Which, of course, sent her traipsing off to the company nurse. And set her quota back another considerable degree. Of course, to make matters worse, Old Personality-Plus Hardwick is forever breathing down the poor girl's neck, making her even more nervous and frazzled. She can't do anything right."

"How sad," Mary commiserated. "Not for faint of heart is sewing factory."

"You said it." Estelle chewed thoughtfully for a few seconds. "I really can't fault Gertie for a lack of effort, though. I think she just tries too hard. It wouldn't surprise me if she ends up going somewhere else, soon, to find a job."

Mary wagged her head, remembering her own difficulties in making the quota. Already it seemed a long time ago.

"Oh!" Estelle brightened. "Speaking of jobs, my big brother was up first thing this morning. Remember he mentioned something about going to talk to his old boss and see if he could get his position back?"

Even as she nodded, Mary wanted to ask more details but couldn't bring herself to pry. She had no idea what kind of work Nelson had done before the war.

"He worked at Lawson Engineering," Estelle went on in her chatty way. "Nelse always dreamed of designing wonderful bridges and great buildings. From the time he was a kid, he filled sketchbooks and drafting tablets with the most incredible drawings. To say nothing of notebooks crammed with all these complicated mathematical equations. He's really quite the brain, you know. Not like his mere mortal sister, who had to study and cram and sweat over every test at school."

Mary smiled to herself at her friend's lowly opinion of herself. But it was not hard at all to envision a youthful Nelson absorbed in his drawings. She only prayed today went well for him, and that he could, in fact, get his position back again. Then his life could start returning to normal. He deserved that much, if not more. A man needed to settle down, get married. . . . Any woman would be proud to have such a fine, smart husband. Her chest rose and fell on a silent sigh.

Just then the factory bell trilled the back-to-work signal. Wadding up their lunch sacks, the girls rose and hurried back to take their places.

"Well, back to the old grind," Estelle quipped. "This little break seems shorter every day. I'm sure glad tomorrow's Tuesday, and we have supper at our house to look forward to."

"Yes," Mary agreed. But inside she'd already decided not to go home with Estelle anymore. She just didn't know how to break the news.

fifteen

How could it be Tuesday morning already? Mary Theresa peered at her alarm clock to determine if it had gone off at the set time. She had no idea when she'd dozed off, having watched hours pass by one after another. Kneading her temples, she padded to the bathroom to wash her face and freshen up. It took a light touch of makeup to cover the grayish circles below her eyes, but Mary hoped the evidence of yet another sleepless night would be less noticeable.

She should have simply told Estelle she wouldn't be coming anymore. But now, her mother would be expecting her, have extra food planned and in the making. It vexed Mary to remember that on previous occasions with Estelle's family she'd taken extra care to choose just the right dress, hoping to look especially nice for them. Or to be more truthful, for Nelson. But even as she acknowledged the fact, she could see the utter futility of such nonsense. What could she have been thinking?

"The problem is, when it comes to Nelson, you forget to think," she lectured herself around her toothbrush. "You forget he deserves much better. Useless daydreams; they must stop."

Yesterday's clouds had been the prelude to another summer storm, and the steady rain which had battered the windows throughout the night would likely continue all day. Intending to choose an outfit that wouldn't spot easily, Mary went to her closet and picked through the lot, finally selecting a charcoal gabardine skirt with a matching cardigan and a plain blouse. Dull enough to match the day and her mood, she mused. After throwing a small lunch together, she bagged it, picked up her purse and umbrella, and left for the trolley.

Amazingly, Estelle's bright face and grin met her from the middle of the streetcar as Mary entered and paid the fare. Returning her friend's smile, she went to join her. "Early today you are."

"I got ready a little quicker than usual, I guess." She grinned. "What a morning, huh? Looks like there'll be no shady bench for lunchtime today."

Mary opened her mouth to respond, but Estelle continued with scarcely a breath. "Hey, wait'll you hear. Dad and a mechanic from our neighborhood rigged Nelse's old car up with a hand clutch, so he can drive now. Isn't that great?"

"Yes. Great." Though she hadn't started out the day with enthusiasm, somehow the good news about Nelson did raise Mary's spirits a little.

"It would appear his old boss will take him back, too. So starting next week, big brother will be a working man again."

"Happy for him I am." But the words were barely out of her mouth before Estelle cut in once more.

"Yeah, he and Dad went out for some practice drives that day and the next. I think they were both amazed at how quickly Nelse picked up applying the clutch with his hand instead of his left foot."

Having no idea what that even meant, Mary only smiled and diverted her attention to the rain-slick world outside the windows. Much as she yearned to know anything and everything about Nelson, she couldn't afford to spend much time thinking about him. . .not when she planned to wangle her way out of having to see him again. The only thing she hadn't figured out was how to tell Estelle. Mary didn't dwell on the anguish she'd incur by letting their beautiful friendship cool. . .but far better to do it that way than to have the truth of her past deal the mortal wound to their relationship. And it would, eventually.

Soon enough, the girls arrived at the factory, took their

stations, and threw themselves into their work. With the doors closed against the dampness, the cavernous interior of the place quickly grew sticky, and amplified the cacophony of noise from all the machines, as well. Mary did her best to ignore the discomfort and concentrate on making the quota back in her own corner.

Something about the stiffness of the new fabric and the way the shirt collars turned out reminded her of her late father, dressed ever so fastidiously, as befitted his position at the university. Mama had taken pride in starching and ironing Papa's white dress shirts just so. And he'd had such plans for his offspring. Mary couldn't help wondering what he would think of his daughter now, so far away from home, slaving away in such a wretched place. The thought brought a sad smile. But at least she was alive. Perhaps it would be enough for him to know she had escaped the horrors that had claimed the rest of their beloved family.

The lunch bell shattered Mary's pensive thoughts. Clipping the threads on the piece she'd just finished, she turned off her machine and plucked her lunch and thermos from the bottom drawer. Instead of losing herself in remembrances of the past, she wished she'd have spent the time rehearsing what to say to Estelle. But it was too late now. She drew a fortifying breath and made the long walk to her friend's station.

"Oh, Mare. Hi," the bubbly brunette sang out as Mary approached. She tapped the machine beside her. "Gertie's out with an infected finger, so you can sit here in your old spot while we eat. It'll be like old times, almost." She unwrapped the food she'd brought and laid it out.

With a nod, Mary tugged out the vacant chair and sank onto it, then reached into her own lunch sack.

"How're those collars coming along?" Estelle teased. "Knowing you, every one that goes through your machine comes out perfect."

"Not always," Mary confessed. "One I hide sometimes."

"I know just what you mean. I've had my bad moments, too. And by the end of the day I'm just anxious to get out of this place and forget about it for awhile." She nibbled a celery stick. "If it weren't for Tuesdays and knowing you'll be coming home with me after work, I'd dread the entire week."

Mary swallowed a chunk of her sandwich without chewing it and regretted it immediately. She grabbed for her tea to help wash it down.

"Is something wrong?" Estelle asked.

It seemed the ideal chance to start manufacturing the excuses she might need to build on later. "I. . .I. . . Not very good I am feeling." It wasn't exactly a lie, Mary reasoned. Doing this to her best friend inflicted more than a little guilt, and she felt positively awful about it.

Especially when she saw Estelle's cheery demeanor collapse before her eyes.

"You're sick? Oh, no. I kind of thought you looked a little tired on the trolley this morning."

Nodding with just a touch more misery than she needed to, Mary wrapped the remainder of her uneaten lunch and tucked it into the bag.

"Well, Mom is really good at fixing what ails people. Maybe when we get home—"

"Please," Mary fudged, "maybe tonight my home is better for me to go."

Her friend's lips sagged at the corners. "Oh, and I so count on your visits." Then her lips softened and lifted with a forced smile. "Oh, well. If I must live without you one week when you're not yourself, I guess I'll get over it. After all, there's always Sunday, right?"

"Yes," Mary agreed, feeling like a skunk. "There is Sunday."

Which gave her a couple days to come up with an excuse to bow out of that, too.

હ⊷

Nelson steered onto a dead-end street to demonstrate how smoothly he could use the hand clutch during a perfect turn-around, then pulled back out onto the busy avenue, merging with the other Wednesday night traffic. The coupe purred like a kitten, and the breeze pouring in through the open windows felt balmy and wonderful. He grinned at Jonathan.

With a futile attempt to smooth his windblown sandy hair, Jon nodded. "Not bad, Buddy. Not bad at all. It's great to see you tooling around again. I was about to give up trying to light a fire under you anymore."

"Yeah, don't remind me what a sap I've been. I'm trying to make up for it."

"So what did it?" Jon probed. "Or maybe I should make that *who*. That pretty little Polish chick? Is she the reason for this new resolve?"

Nelson's irritated glance caught his pal's suggestive wink. "Why is it, whenever you come around, it's Mary Theresa this, Mary Theresa that? I do have my own life, you know, and did even before she got here."

"Well, pardon me," Jon snapped back. "I used to be able to kid around with you in the old days." His tone gentled. "It's just that you've started coming back to life lately, and as far as I know, she does happen to be the only new factor in the equation."

Nelson shook his head in chagrin. "You're right. I didn't mean to fly off the handle. I'm being a jerk. And right after prayer meeting, too. Guess I should've paid more attention to that sermon."

"So," Jon began a little more cautiously, "are you saying she is or isn't a factor in all this? She does have supper at your house every week, doesn't she? And Stella says Mary's started tagging along on Sunday morning with you guys, too. Are you telling me you're not interested?"

Passing a slower vehicle which pulled out into the road, Nelson shrugged. "I don't know. And that's the truth."

"What do you mean? We used to talk, Nelse. Open up."

Conceding that his friend was right, Nelson tried to imagine putting his feelings into words when he still had to figure things out for himself. He inhaled a troubled breath and released it. But he really did need to talk to somebody, and who better than his best friend? He finally took the plunge. "I thought at first there might be some kind of. . .attraction there—"

"On your part, or hers?"

"Both," Nelson admitted. "The first time Mary Theresa came home with Stella she seemed like a scared rabbit. But then she started warming up. She's the one who came walking with me when I needed to get used to my peg, and all. And we'd talk a little. She's. . .got a lot of problems, you know?"

Jonathan gave a thoughtful nod. "She came from overseas after the war, right? She must've seen a lot."

"I'm sure she did. Mary doesn't talk much about it, but I thought she was starting to open up with me."

"Starting?"

"Yeah. Told me a couple little things I don't think she's even told Stella, or I'd have heard them already." He smirked.

A chuckle burst from the passenger side, and Jon's grin took awhile to disappear. "So what happened? Why'd you say you 'thought' she was opening up?"

Nelson grimaced. "Because all of a sudden she made a U-turn. Last time she came over, on Sunday, she gets this sudden headache. Then last night, when we all expected her to come for supper, she begged off, saying she was sick. Well, it'll be Sunday again in a couple more days. If she gives Stella another convenient little excuse, it won't take a genius to figure. It's me she's avoiding."

Jon tipped his head, doubt written all over his face. "Not necessarily."

"On the other hand," Nelson continued, "it's just as well. I'm heading back to Lawson's come Monday morning. To my old job."

"So I hear. That's terrific."

He nodded. "Figure I'll have enough on my hands with getting back into that routine, keeping my car running, going to church. Guess I don't need another complication right now. Later there'll be plenty of time to find some gal willing to put up with me and—" He tapped his artificial leg and shrugged. "So for now. . ."

"Whatever you say, Buddy." Jonathan clammed up and looked out his side window.

The sudden silence didn't sit well with Nelson. He took a different tack. "So what's with you and Sis? Gonna give her another shot?"

Jonathan winced. "Who knows? Think she's ready?"

"Only one way to find out."

"I suppose."

Funny how much easier it seemed to give advice than to take it, Nelson mused. But something had definitely changed with Mary Theresa. Ever since they'd gone to church. Since he caught a glimpse of her tattoo. The way she kept it hidden, a person would think being thrown into a concentration camp was something to be ashamed of. Something that was her fault.

Or was it him. . .him and his leg? Maybe she thought it too painful a reminder of a time she'd prefer to forget.

Whichever it happened to be, Sunday would either be the beginning. . .or the end.

First, however, there was something he needed to do.

sixteen

Curled up on her couch with her fingers wrapped around a cup of hot tea, Mary lost herself in the quiet music playing on the radio. In a little while she'd run a bubble bath and soak away the weariness of the day, but for now it was enough to relax and clear her mind of all troubling thoughts regarding letting go of Estelle. . .and even sadder, Nelson. She'd grown so easily fond of his rich voice, of kindnesses so like his sister's. Their sweet friendship was among her greatest treasures, and her visits to that loving home, the brightest spots in her world.

A few light taps sounded on the front door.

Startled, Mary almost spilled her tea as she jumped to her feet. She hadn't heard anyone come up the steps. She set the half-empty cup on the lamp table and padded to answer the summons. "Who is outside?"

A pause. "It's me. Nelson."

Nelson! Mary swallowed her surprise, then unlocked and opened the door.

A sheepish grin met her in the dim lamplight spilling out the opening. "I hope it's not too late. I happened to be passing your street and thought I'd drop by. I have something to give you."

Words failed her. Should she invite him in? Was that proper? Or wise?

"May I come in? I promise I won't stay long."

"O–of course," she stammered. Hoping she'd made the right choice, she stepped aside.

"Nice little place," he said with a disarming smile as he glanced around the small living room with an expression of approval.

"Thank you. With decorating Estelle helped me."

"Ah, yes, the famous shopping trip. She talked of nothing else for days."

"I, too, had fun."

He nodded.

"Some tea you would like? I am having." Gesturing toward the couch and her own cup, she gave a questioning shrug.

"Sure. Thanks." With that, he settled into the adjacent slip-covered chair.

Mary hastened to the kitchenette and took a second cup and saucer from her drainer. Once she'd poured the tea and added a few cookies to a plate, she brought them to her guest. "Are you taking sugar or cream?"

"Black is fine, thank you."

Reclaiming her seat, Mary did her best to relax, despite the fact that her pulse insisted on doing silly things.

Nothing seemed to fluster Estelle's brother. He raised the cup to his lips, his gaze riveted to her as an instrumental rendition of "Something To Remember You By" filled the silence.

She wished she'd turned the music down or even off. It lent a kind of intimacy to the moment she didn't feel she had a right to.

"We've been missing you lately."

"Yes, I–I'm sorry." She fluttered a hand, a hapless substitute for an explanation.

"Anyway," he went on, "I saw something in a bookstore near where I work and thought you might find it useful." Reaching into an inner pocket of his jacket, he withdrew a gilt-edged book and leaned forward to hand it to her.

"Always gifts you are bringing," Mary said softly, then gazed down at it. She gasped. "A Bible! In Polish!" Her mouth parted in shock as she looked up at him again, her heart swelling in response to yet another display of his thoughtfulness.

"I know it can't be easy for you to muddle through King

James's English," he said, his tone gentle. "Even we have problems understanding some of those old words. But I thought maybe if you could read in your own language, it might help you find clearer meaning to the verses."

"Oh, Nelson," she breathed. "Too kind, too generous you are. I will love this. How much you cannot know."

With a gratified grin, he drained the remainder of the tea in his cup, then stood. "Well, that's all I hoped. Maybe sometime we can talk over a few passages again. I enjoyed the questions you came up with. They made me think."

Mary felt her cheeks warming under his scrutiny. "Maybe the day comes when I not bother you with questions," she murmured, grateful beyond words as she rose to her feet to walk him to the door.

Reaching the tiny entry, Nelson hesitated, his hand closing around the knob without turning it as his eyes made a leisurely perusal of her flushed face. "I hope we never reach that point, Mary Theresa. I really do." Then with a last heart-stopping grin, he left.

Mary sagged against the closed door, fighting tears as she turned the lock after him. Such a loss he would be.

≈

If Mary Theresa imagined that disappointing Estelle had been tough to do on Tuesday, her dread of going to work on Friday about doubled that discomfort. She knew that with its arrival would come lunch with Estelle, as would the inevitable discussion leading to the Sunday service. Mary wracked her brain trying to fabricate a plausible way to evade spending time with the Thomases—after she'd practically promised to start going to church regularly with them. She hadn't mentioned Nelson's visit a few nights ago, and since Estelle hadn't, either, Mary could only assume he hadn't said anything himself. Which was fortunate.

Facing herself in the mirror, she practiced maintaining an

even expression while mouthing a few pretexts. "Cramping I have. My cycle. . ." No, not that. "A big tooth in back is. . ." Mary shook her head in disgust. "How about the truth? I cannot come because your brother I lo—"

Even without finishing the word, the certitude of what she'd almost said shook her down to her toes. . .it wasn't a fabrication. Despite all the noble plans she'd made to remain aloof from Nelson Thomas, to save him and his family from her wretched past, the unthinkable had happened. Mary had grown to love her best friend's brother.

Now more than ever, she knew she could never return to Estelle's home. What if her feelings somehow emblazoned themselves across her face or radiated from her eyes. . .or worse yet, came tripping out of her mouth? How humiliating it would be to reveal her whole heart, only to have it and her impossible dreams crushed forever. To see the affection that precious family had shown her turn to horror and loathing would be much more shattering than all the agonies she had endured at Ravensbruck.

Straightening her shoulders, Mary Theresa reaffirmed her decision to withdraw from Estelle and her family. . .or at least the family and Nelson. Working with Estelle, she would still have some measure of friendship with her. Or so Mary hoped. She could not bear to hurt the girl any more than necessary.

To avoid running into her before working hours, Mary dressed quickly and caught an earlier trolley, then loitered out of sight in the solitary confines of the lavatory until the start bell.

If ever there had been a shorter morning at Olympic Sewing Factory, Mary Theresa didn't know when it could have occurred. When the lunch signal pierced the air, only the stack of completed collars in her basket belied the notion that she'd barely sat down to work.

She drew a cleansing breath and affected her most casual

expression. Then, gathering her lunch, she went to meet her friend, and the two of them exited the factory.

"Gertrude's back at work," Estelle commented as they sat eating on their bench a few moments later. "Her finger's still bandaged, but she's determined to stick this out and prove to Hardwick that she can do her job."

"Good. Glad for her I am."

"Me, too. It seems a new employee needs that kind of gumption to make a quota. You had it, and look at you. You've been promoted already." Smiling, Estelle finished the last of her hard-boiled egg.

Mary shook her head. Right from the first, it had felt more like a demotion than an advancement, being moved so far away from Estelle, electric machine or no. After all, it only happened because some other girl had quit. Noticing a gray pigeon inching tentatively closer to her shoe, she carefully broke some crumbs from the cookie she'd been nibbling and let them fall from her fingers.

"I've been asked to sing a solo this Sunday," Estelle said, her eyes soft as she watched the birds coming to Mary's feast. "Well, actually, the choir will back me up with some ooohs and aaaahs in several measures of the song. But it's one of my very favorites: 'The Old Rugged Cross.' Do you know it?"

"I do not think so."

"Well, then, you're in for a treat. Pardon my modesty," she giggled.

Mary drew a deep breath. "I. . .on Sunday I cannot come."

"You can't?" One of the few actual frowns she'd ever seen on Estelle's face creased her smooth forehead. "Really? I thought you enjoyed coming with us last week."

"I did."

"Is it because we're Protestants? And you were uncomfortable in our style of worship?"

That would make it easier, Mary reasoned. Only it wasn't true. "Not that. The Chudziks I want to visit," she blurted. And once it popped out, the idea sounded quite good, so she added to it. "Veronica and Christine I am missing."

Estelle's delicate features smoothed out again, like waves at sea after a storm had passed. "Oh, of course you would, after living with them all those months. I should have anticipated that."

Breathing an inward sigh of relief, Mary didn't feel quite as bad now herself. She tossed a few more crumbs to the birds.

"Well, we'll expect you as usual then, on Tuesday. Okay?"

Mary knew she just had to tell Estelle she would no longer come home with her at all. Ever. There was no getting around it. She opened her mouth and drew a breath to get the words out.

"You can't say no this time," Estelle cut in, her dark eyes sparkling with mischief. "It's my birthday."

Mary's spirits plummeted to the sidewalk. Once again she could not refuse.

28

"This is just the loveliest surprise," Mrs. Chudzik gushed when Mary Theresa showed up on their doorstep. "If you had a telephone, we could have called and taken you to Mass with us."

"Next time, maybe," Mary hedged, easing out of the woman's embrace. No sense alluding to having missed church altogether.

As she followed her inside, two sets of footsteps skittered toward them, and Veronica and Christine let out a squeal. "Mary! Mary's here!" And they surrounded her with loving arms.

"We were just about to sit down to dinner," their mother announced. "There's plenty. Are you hungry?"

"A little," Mary confessed. "May I help?"

"No, everything's on the table. All we need is you. We want to hear all about how you're doing out on your own, how your job is going, what friends you've been making."

With an appreciative glance around the familiar surroundings of her first home in America, Mary followed her two "little sisters" to dinner, trying very hard to appear happy.

"Sissy and I have started taking dance classes," Christine said during dinner.

"How nice," Mary said. "Fun it must be."

"I used to take ballet when I was little," Veronica explained. "But I've always wanted to learn tap. We're giving a recital soon, and you can come see us dance."

Mary nodded, enjoying hearing the girls' experiences again.

"And how is your job going?" their mother asked.

"Good. Everything I like but supervisor. This woman I must show." Mary got up and offered an imitation of a perpetually scowling Mrs. Hardwick skulking through the rows of sewing machines, an imaginary magnifying glass poised to search out flaws in people's work.

The family roared with laughter, and Mary couldn't help but get caught up in it herself. For a few moments, it almost felt as though she'd never left them to go off on her own.

"Child," stout little Mr. Chudzik said from the head of the table, "it does our hearts good to see how well you've adjusted to life in this country. If I'm not mistaken, even your English seems to be getting clearer." He rested his elbows on the armrests of his chair and nodded approvingly.

"Thank you. Hard I try, to sound like others. I do not think always in Polish now."

"Oh! Speaking of Polish," his wife gasped, placing a pudgy hand to her heart, "a letter came for you the other day. I almost forgot."

"I know where you put it, Mother," Veronica said, and

jumping up from the table, she bolted to retrieve the envelope from the parlor.

Mary Theresa held her breath, wondering who could have written to her.

The postmark revealed the missive had come from Florida, which added even more to the mystery. But then the return address caught her eye. "Rahel! From my friend, Rahel!" she exclaimed, delighted beyond words. She smiled and tucked the mail into her skirt pocket. "For later I must save."

It seemed to take forever until the meal ended and the dishes had been washed and put away. And all the while, Mary could feel Rahel's letter in her pocket. From time to time she touched it with her fingers just to be sure it didn't disappear. But, Florida! Why Florida?

Finally, the Chudziks drove her home and waved goodbye. Mary slipped inside and ran up the stairs to her apartment. Then she tore into the message from her Jewish friend:

Dearest Marie Therese,
    I hope this letter finds you. I have been trying for a long time to learn where you are. I wrote to Josep and Ania for help, and they told me they believe you went to live with one of their American contacts named Chudzik. I am trying them first. If I do not hear from you, I will write to Josep for other names.

Still overwhelmed at having received this unexpected word from her dear friend, Mary smiled to herself. Rahel had not changed. The determination which had enabled her to survive the death camp would likely see her through the rest of her life, as well. She returned her attention to the pages in her hand, realizing how strange it seemed to be reading Polish again after having been so thoroughly immersed in the English language since her arrival in New York.

There is so much to tell you, I do not know where to begin. The ship I took to Palestine was not permitted to dock. Too many refugees already, they told us, so my grand plan of settling there and making jewelry did not come to be. Many places I went after that. Too many to write. But at last I came to Miami.

I work now for a family named Goldberg, in their store. The owner, Mr. Goldberg, likes the pieces I make, so he lets me design others. But most amazing is that even with a Jewish name and heritage, he and his wife have become Christians. They believe Jesus to be the Messiah promised centuries before His birth in Bethlehem. It reminds me of hearing the Bible at the camp. I am starting to believe it was true, all those things we heard.

Mary's eyes widened as she reread that paragraph. Rahel, becoming a Christian believer! An added sense of joy filled her. She had begun to accept those teachings herself but had never brought herself to share that with anyone. She read on:

It seems strange to live in a place where there is peace. Peace all around, and now peace growing inside my heart. But I am very lonely here. How I wish my family were alive to enjoy this with me. That is why I am writing. I feel as if you are my family now. My sister. And I think how wonderful it would be if we could live in the same place, be happy together.

If you get my letter, please write to me. I know you might like being in New York and not want to leave there. That is fine. But think about how much fun we could have together. It is always warm in Florida. We could learn to swim in the ocean. Even if you cannot come to live here, you could still visit me. I long

*to learn about you and your life in America. I will wait
to hear from you.*

Your friend always,
Rahel

Hugging the letter to her breast, Mary Theresa laid her head against the back of the couch. How very precious to know that Rahel was safe and doing well, and in the trade she loved. So many prayers had been answered. And Rahel wanted Mary to join her. That would take some consideration. Florida was a long way from New York.

It would also be a long way from Nelson. That would be hard.

But to stay in Manhattan and face the possibility of running into him, knowing all the while that nothing could ever come of it. . .that would be much harder still.

Perhaps, she mused, this might be the solution for her dilemma.

seventeen

A late summer breeze ruffled the hem of Estelle's green-and-white-striped cotton dress and toyed with a wisp of shiny sable hair. Mary Theresa watched her brush it away from her face to munch the ham and cheese sandwich she'd brought for lunch. "I thought today would never get here," Estelle remarked.

Beside her on their bench, Mary only wished she shared that sentiment. For her, the days leading up to this one seemed to have wings. There'd been nothing she could do to slow its coming. *And after those well-laid plans to stay away from the Thomases, too,* she thought scornfully. All for naught. Somehow she would have to weather one more long evening at Estelle's.

Thankfully, her friend didn't pick up on her angst. "This is the first birthday in ages that my whole family will be together. Nelson missed the last couple, being off at war, you know."

Mary just nodded. Nelson. How would she survive the upcoming hours in his presence, knowing how she felt about him?

"Do people celebrate birthdays in Poland?" Estelle asked casually.

Sloughing off her troubled thoughts, Mary tried for an outward show of enthusiasm. "Yes. This custom we have. But now, most have no means to a celebration of the day."

"Oh, I'm sorry. Well, Mom always bakes a special cake when it's somebody's birthday and usually makes some really thoughtful gift we had no inkling she had in the works. Once in awhile it'll be something store-bought." She stopped suddenly and glanced at Mary. "When is your birthday, Mare? I've never asked you that."

"Sixteen, of April."

"Oh, rats. We'll have to wait over half a year for it to get here. I just know my mom will want to make you a birthday cake, too. You're like part of the family."

Even as Mary tried to ignore the pang of guilt that followed her friend's last comment, part of her still sought an escape. Something to prevent her from having to go through with this. But the friendship she and Estelle shared meant far too much to her, and Mary just didn't have the heart to disappoint her. Not on the day of her birth. She would get through this somehow. . .this one last time before she left here forever. Could she muster enough courage to move to Florida?

Mary's thoughts naturally drifted to Rahel. She'd read and reread the treasured letter so many times over the last two nights, she nearly had it memorized. She'd even started on a reply, wanting it to be as informative as possible without actually making a commitment. But now, anticipating the swift arrival of yet another family get-together at Estelle's, the notion of going somewhere far away grew in appeal.

A pair of pigeons cooed in the background while a particularly venturesome one pecked its way through bread crumbs at Mary's feet.

"I know you had a swell time with your host family on Sunday," Estelle said, gazing at the birds, "but will they be expecting you every week now? Maybe to go to church with them again?"

"That we did not discuss," Mary answered truthfully, then brightened. "Guess what? A letter they had for me. From Polish friend, Rahel Dubinsky." An easier smile came to her lips.

"Really? How interesting. Had she written you before?"

Mary shook her head. "Contact we lost when to Holy Land

she sailed and to America I come."

"Well, how splendid that you've found each other again." Estelle grew pensive. "It must be lovely to be in that part of the world. Imagine walking on the very roads and paths the Lord walked along. Or climbing hills where He must have preached to the crowds, seeing the Sea of Galilee. What a feeling that would be."

"Palestine is not taking her. In Florida is Rahel now. To live there."

"Oh." Estelle tilted her head with a puzzled frown. "I'm sure it must be nice there, too."

Mary nodded. "She. . .wants for me to visit." *Maybe stay forever,* she added silently.

"Too bad you have a job here," Estelle crooned. "Old Hardwick has a conniption when any of her workers dare to take time off—except in cases of death, of course." She snickered. "And even then, it had better be their own. She'd have to allow at least a half-day in that case."

Mary smiled but did not answer.

With the lunch bell ending their noon break, the girls rose and brushed off their skirts, then returned to their workplaces.

Hoping to keep her mind off how swiftly the afternoon would end, Mary threw herself into her work. She'd found the making of collars incredibly simple, and the process had so quickly become automatic, she imagined she could do them with her eyes closed. While adding steadily to her stacks of finished pieces, she mulled over her answer to Rahel. Anything to keep her mind off how much she longed to see Nelson and be with him.

Mary knew the supervisor would never permit an extended absence to a relatively new employee, and she had not earned any vacation time. In order to go to Florida to visit Rahel, she would have to quit her job. And if she quit her job, she might as well make the move permanent. Could she bear that?

But. . .could she bear not to?

All too soon, the quitting bell startled her from her dilemma. Gathering the completed articles together, she turned them in, then went to meet Estelle.

And face the dreaded gathering which lay ahead.

"At last!" Her friend exclaimed, bubbly as ever. "What a long day, huh? Well, it's finally over. Now we can go home."

As the girls disembarked the trolley at Estelle's stop, the setting sun cast a soft peach blush over the rows of tenement houses lining the street, blending variegated textures and colors into a softer palette. Mary's gaze wandered along the tiny yards that had become so familiar in the short time she had been coming to dinner with her friend. She'd chosen a few favorites among them, knew which ones had the loveliest rose-bushes, the prettiest curtains, the sweetest children. Knowing she wouldn't pass this way again after today, she found herself committing the familiar sights to memory. She'd call them to mind often, when she went to live with Rahel.

But one, tucked between a unit with asbestos siding and another trimmed with brick face, would forever stand out above the rest. As Mary approached the Thomas home, she drank in the neat pale yellow exterior and tidy window boxes overflowing with brilliant geraniums. She imagined she would hear the slap of that screen door in her sleep, recall the good-natured banter that filled the rooms, smell the delicious meals Estelle's mother inevitably prepared.

"Mmm," Estelle murmured as they went inside. "Chocolate. I knew she'd bake my favorite cake." She looped her purse strap over a hook on the hall tree, and Mary followed suit.

"Well, well," Nelson grinned, coming to his feet from the easy chair. "If it isn't the birthday gal. Hi, Squirt. Mary."

Estelle sent him a sisterly grin.

"Hello." Unable to sustain his warm gaze, Mary lowered her lashes and smiled. It wouldn't do for him to read her feelings. She schooled her features into what she hoped was polite reserve.

"Dad home yet?" Estelle asked.

"Nope, but he called a few seconds ago to say he's on his way."

Just then Mrs. Thomas breezed in, her cheeks rosy as the pink print housedress she wore. "Oh, hello, girls. We're so glad you could join us, Mary. And don't you look pretty. We missed having you around here lately."

"Hello, and thank you." Smiling, Mary did her best to stifle a flush. She hadn't especially planned to dress for the occasion, and had donned a dark floral print skirt and complementing blouse. Obviously, even the simplest outfits in her wardrobe reflected Mrs. Chudzik's good taste and Veronica's eye for fashion. Mary had never taken off the fine chain Rahel gave her, except to add a crucifix to the Star of David. Though most days it remained out of sight, today it did not. "Delicious, something smells," she said, hoping to divert everyone's attention away from her.

"That would be the chicken and dumplings Stella requested," Mrs. Thomas supplied. "Birthday people choose the menu on their special day. It's kind of a tradition we adopted over the years." She glanced to Estelle. "Your father should be home any moment, Dear, so we'll be eating shortly."

"Great, Mom. And it does smell good—as usual."

She stepped nearer and gave her daughter a hug. Then with a light laugh, she embraced Mary as well, patting her back. "My two girls."

Mary had to swallow a huge lump in her throat but did manage a smile.

"Think I hear Dad," Nelson said, moving to the window. "Yeah, that's him." Turning back, he rubbed his palms together and grinned. "Finally. I've had to sit here smelling all this stuff ever since I got home from work. A man can take only so much, you know."

The usual clomping up the outside steps brought Mr. Thomas through the door, which clapped shut behind him. "Hi, all," he said with a glance that encompassed everyone. "Happy birthday, Snooks. Nice to see you here, Mary. Smells like supper's waiting."

"It is," his wife announced. "Go wash up, and we can start right in."

Not needing instruction as they all filed into the dining room, Mary Theresa claimed the spot which had been hers from the first. She chanced a quick look across at Nelson while he sat down, and he grinned, sending the butterflies inside her into chaotic flight. Did he have to be wearing the brown-checked shirt she liked so much?

"Well," his father said, his bifocaled glance making a circuit and settling on Mary, "the whole family is together again." Immediately he bowed his head. "Dear Lord, we are so blessed. Thank You for Your boundless love and provision for our needs. Thank You for Stella and the bright spot she is in all our lives. Grant a special blessing at this special time set aside to commemorate the day You gave her to us. And bless our Mary, as well. Thank You for bringing her back to us. We give You our praise. In Your Son's name, we pray. Amen."

Too caught up in the touching grace to echo his amen, Mary crossed herself and opened her eyes, more than aware of Nelson's focus on her.

"This does look luscious, my dear," Mr. Thomas said, gazing down at the china tureen all but overflowing with its bounty. "If everyone will pass plates, I'll see that you get served."

Welcoming even that small diversion, Mary gave hers to Estelle to pass on. Within moments, a generous portion of the chicken mixture and a fluffy dumpling came back. She couldn't believe the cloudlike softness as she cut into the moist, steamed dough. . .and the taste of it and the accompanying stew seemed like a dream. "Very good this is," she told Mrs. Thomas in all sincerity.

"Why, thank you, Dear. I'm glad you like it."

"How was work today, Nelse?" his father asked. "Starting to fit in yet?"

He chuckled. "I kind of feel like the new kid on the block, actually. But things are coming back. I can connect the names to the right faces pretty well already. Mr. Gavin's letting me go slow. Yesterday and today, he had me refining some blueprints for a project he has in the works. Shouldn't be long before I'll be going out to job sites with the rest of the guys."

Stella shook her head. "I never could figure out what all those lines and diagrams mean." She turned to Mary. "Engineers and architects can look at that stuff and somehow envision an entire building, basement to roof."

"We are geniuses. Just plain geniuses," he quipped, forking a carrot chunk to his mouth.

"And how about you girls?" Mr. Thomas went on. "Quotas coming along at the factory?"

Estelle nodded, then shot a glare to her brother. "Of course, we do more than merely scribble stuff on paper, like some geniuses I know. But our favorite time is lunch hour." She returned her attention to her father. "That's when we get to put aside our grand endeavors and go sit in the fresh air with the pigeons. They like Mary."

"My food they like," she corrected. "Watching them is. . . nice."

"I'd imagine the feeling is mutual," Nelson teased.

Meeting those merry light brown eyes, Mary almost couldn't swallow.

"Anyone care for more?" Mr. Thomas offered, the ladle ready in his hand.

"No thanks, Daddy," Estelle said. "I need to save room for cake."

Nelson, however, didn't hesitate in the least, and handed over his plate, his eyebrows waggling in a comical fashion. "Some of us are just getting started."

At the close of the meal, Mary and Mrs. Thomas cleared away the main course while Estelle reveled in her lofty position as the birthday girl. Then Mary returned with a stack of cake plates, and the lady of the house brought in a triple-layer cake, iced in white frosting and decorated with colored sprinkles and lighted birthday candles.

"Good grief! A regular inferno," Nelson teased. "You're gettin' old, Sis."

She gave a playful kick under the table.

But when the others broke into "Happy Birthday," Mary could only mouth the unfamiliar words. She had to smile when Estelle made an elaborate display of blowing out those twenty-two rapidly melting candles.

Mary couldn't remember enjoying a moister chocolate cake in her life, and felt so full she had to force down the mound of chocolate ice cream on the side. From the sparkle in Estelle's eyes, she sensed her friend had chosen the flavor in her honor.

Finally, dessert dishes were whisked away, and a small pile of presents replaced them at the center of the table. Mary got caught up in Estelle's delight over the bounty of thoughtful gifts. . .a hand-embroidered blouse her mom had made, a new alarm clock from both parents. She held her breath when her friend opened the present she'd brought, hoping it, too, would please her.

"Oh, Mare. Thank you. I've been needing a new silk scarf. It's just beautiful and my favorite shade of green." Estelle reached over and hugged her.

"You have one more thing, Squirt," Nelson reminded her, nudging a small gift her way.

Mary watched Estelle's eyes grow misty as she gazed inside the narrow jeweler's box and drew from the cotton lining a tiny gold cross suspended on a delicate Figaro chain. "Oh, Nelse." She sprang up and ran to hug his neck from behind. "You remembered I broke my other one. Thank you."

"Anytime, Sis," he grinned, patting the arm nearly choking him.

Estelle straightened. "And thank you, everybody. This has been my best birthday ever. I love you all."

Against poignant memories of her own childhood birthdays, Mary's heart ached at the atmosphere of love in this home. . .and the priceless joys that had been ripped away from her so long ago. She could hardly get beyond the clog of emotion in her throat.

"Well, Mary, dear," Mrs. Thomas said, providing a most welcome distraction, "it looks as if you and I will be dealing with the aftermath."

She took a deep breath and plastered on a smile. "Fine. To help I like." Detaching herself from old griefs she could not afford to dwell on, Mary stood and began gathering the discarded wrapping paper and ribbons, wondering if her relief was obvious to anyone else.

She braved a shy glance at Nelson and felt somehow encouraged to see a gentle smile on his lips. And Mary knew she would miss that sight most of all. . .

eighteen

Nelson began taking stock of Mary Theresa from the moment she and Stella arrived, weighing her expressions, tone of voice, her manner, the way she responded to questions and comments. He'd been convinced she'd quit coming around because of him, but he had to find out for sure. He figured if he waited long enough, watched closely enough, she'd trip up somehow, and the truth he sought would be evident. Perhaps painfully so.

But, man, the girl was good. Whenever she knew she was the center of attention, she appeared completely composed, ever so polite, and typically pleasant. Her smile seemed genuine. Obviously she felt real affection for Estelle and their parents, and even offered Nelson a few smiles that looked sincere. But those other times. . .when she didn't know the microscope was focused on her, that's when Nelson caught brief flashes of sadness in her eyes. A sadness so profound it seemed almost tangible. And it did unspeakable things to his insides.

Seated in the parlor after supper, with his father reading the evening paper in his overstuffed chair, Nelson could hear the good-natured banter drifting from the kitchen. He pictured Estelle perched on the step stool while Mary Theresa and Mom did the dishes. Sure sounded like a happy enough group. Maybe his instincts were wrong. But if they were, it would be the first time.

Still mulling over the events of the evening, he turned the radio on and searched the dial for music, then adjusted the volume down.

Francis Langford's "Harbor Lights" flowed smoothly and

low in the background as the ladies finally left the drudgery and came to join the menfolk. Mom picked up her knitting and took her usual spot in the cushioned rocking chair by the fireplace, while his sister and Mary chose opposite ends of the couch. Stella immediately leaned forward to the birthday gifts she'd left on the coffee table and began examining them, this time more closely.

"This scarf will look so pretty with my winter coat," she said breathlessly, running the emerald silk through her fingers. "I can hardly wait for the cooler weather to come."

"In New York are the winters cold, like in Poland?" Mary asked.

"Oh, we may get a few blizzards that are real doozies," she replied. "But, fortunately, here in Manhattan the weather can be pretty mild, a good part of the time. At least now that big brother's around, I won't get stuck shoveling all the snow, this year." She crimped her nose at him.

"Hmm," he returned in stride. "I was thinking of digging out my crutches, come winter. . . ."

"Ha. That's what you think. I turned them into firewood just the other day."

"If you did, you'll regret it."

Looking from one to the other, Mary laughed softly.

Dad peered over the top of his newspaper and nodded to Mom. "I think we just relinquished our peace and quiet to the younger generation. How about we seek solitude in the kitchen? Sure could go for a cup of coffee, maybe another slice of that cake?"

"I think I can accommodate you, Love." Putting aside her project, Mom rose with him, and they traipsed down the hall. The door swished shut behind them.

"Well, apparently we've perfected the art of clearing a room," Nelson said with a wry grin.

"Time for me to go home, I think," Mary said tentatively.

"Just let me make a quick trip upstairs," Stella said. "I'll only be a moment."

Nelson saw Mary's blue green eyes widen as she watched after his sister. Then she settled back against the couch.

A few measures of an introduction, and Jo Stafford's rich voice issued from the speaker. "I'll be seeing you in all the old familiar places. . . ."

Mary's lips curved into a bittersweet smile. She reached to the jeweler's box on the coffee table and took out Stella's necklace, fingering the delicate cross. "Very pretty," she said, her words barely audible.

"I kinda thought she'd like it."

Mary moistened her lips, then hesitated, drew a breath, and spoke. "Why do Protestants wear plain the cross? The death of Jesus they do not like remembering?"

Turning the song down another notch, Nelson met her gaze. "Oh, we remember it, all right. It's a precious thought to know the Lord of Creation became a man and died for our sins. But you see, the story didn't stop there. The fact that He rose again three days later is what's amazing. It's the basis for all our hope. The empty cross is a reminder that all who come to Him will live again one day with Him in heaven."

She appeared to consider his words, then replaced the jewelry in its box. "For good people that is," she said softly. "People who do not sin."

"We all sin, Mary Theresa. Ever since the Garden of Eden. No one is good. The only way any of us can be sure where we'll spend eternity is to ask for God to forgive us and to accept the free gift of salvation He provided through His Son's death on the cross."

"But. . .my past you do not know," she whispered. "Things I have done. No one could forgive such things."

Astounded that she could be so hard on herself, Nelson prayed for wisdom before he answered. "God can, Mary. He promises that though our sins be as scarlet, He will make them white as snow. Here, I'll show you." Plucking his Bible from the lamp table beside his chair, Nelson got up and crossed to the couch. Sitting a respectful distance from her, he showed her the passage in Isaiah and waited for her to read it. "He also promises that no one who comes to Him will be turned away."

"Too bad are some things."

"Nothing, little one, is too bad."

"You are sure of this?"

"Sure enough to bet the ranch on it. God cannot lie." Taking a tract from inside the cover, he gave it to her. "Here, Mary. Keep this, and read it at your leisure. If you'd like to know for certain that you have peace with God, there's a sample prayer on back. But you can make up your own prayer instead, if you prefer. It's not the words that count; it's the heart behind them."

Those troubled eyes raised to his, and they brimmed with trust. "Much Bible I have read already, now that I am reading in Polish. I. . .this peace I would like now," she whispered.

With the greatest joy he had ever experienced, Nelson took the hand of the woman he loved and knelt beside her while she prayed.

⁂

There were no words to describe the lightness of her spirit when Mary Theresa allowed Nelson to assist her to her feet after her prayer. She felt as if a great weight had been removed from her being.

He looped an arm around her shoulder and hugged her. "Welcome to God's family."

She could have hugged him back. Almost. But one conviction still remained. God had forgiven and accepted her. . .but she was still the same person, with the same past. People would not be so forgiving. She braved a smile through moist eyes and eased out of his chaste embrace.

Estelle came tripping downstairs just then, humming to herself.

"I'll let you tell people your good news whenever you're ready," Nelson whispered, moving away.

"Okay," Estelle sang out, entering the room. "We can drive Mary home now."

"Drive?" Mary echoed. "Trolley is fine."

Nelson grinned. "No sense hoofing up the street anymore, when I've got a perfectly good car sitting right outside. You'll be safe. . .I've been practicing. And Stella will come, too."

Unsure, Mary looked to her friend and watched her nod. "Well, okay," she said in her best American. "But thank you and good-bye I must first say, to your parents." She couldn't possibly leave here without doing that. Not with her future plans to consider. Those had not changed.

Moments later, the threesome headed out front to Nelson's coupe. The girls got into the backseat, while Nelson took his place and started the motor. "Hang on to your hats, ladies," he teased over his shoulder.

Mary darted an alarmed glance to Estelle but received only a reassuring pat on the arm. "Don't mind him. He's just feeling his oats now that he can tool around town at a whim."

As he pulled away from the house, Mary settled back and relaxed, watching the passing scenes in the fading twilight.

"Nelse?" Estelle asked before they'd gone half a mile.

"Yeah?"

"Could we stop at Mickey's for a root beer float?"

"What? After all that cake and ice cream at the house? You gotta be kidding."

"No, I'm not," she insisted. "Please? Can we? I'm dying for a root beer float. It is my birthday, remember."

He let out an exasperated huff. "Sisters."

"Is that a yes?" she asked hopefully.

"Yeah." But his wagging head showed his disdain.

Mary, too, thought it incredible that slender Estelle, who rarely consumed her whole bag lunch at work, could possibly yearn for something else after the huge cooked meal and birthday desserts. But it didn't matter all that much. Surely he'd drop her off before they went to Mickey's, wherever that was.

But her street whizzed by without Nelson even slowing down, let alone turning into it. Captive that she was, she held her peace. What other choice did she have?

Mickey's Soda Shoppe, she discovered, turned out to be a charming ice cream parlor not far from Woolworth's, right around the corner from a movie theater. No doubt most of its clientele consisted of young people who frequented the theater and came after the shows.

Nelson parked in front of the establishment, and they exited the car for the restaurant.

Mary couldn't help but gawk at the red-and-white-striped cushions on white wrought-iron chairs surrounding a smattering of tables. . .all the more striking on the black-and-white linoleum floor. A jukebox in one corner blared a lively new song she'd never heard before as they strode to a table in the far corner.

A petite blond waitress in a ruffled white apron and black dress brought menus, then left.

They barely had a chance to open and study them before a familiar voice interrupted. "Well, well. Fancy meeting you guys here."

"Jon!" Nelson exclaimed. "What brings you to Mickey's?"

His mischievous grin split his long face. "Oh, just had a hankering for some ice cream. Hi, Mary. Hi, Birthday Doll." His blue eyes locked on Estelle's.

Mary slanted a glance at her friend and caught an uncharacteristic blush. And a smile the girl couldn't seem to contain.

Nelson, obviously on to something, tucked his chin at his tall, sandy-haired friend, then at his sister. "Okay, what's up?"

Estelle, all innocence by now, only shrugged.

But Jon pulled up a chair. "So, what is it? Hot fudge sundaes all around? Chocolate milk shakes? Or do we go whole hog on the banana splits?" He winked at Estelle.

"We were about to have root beer floats," she supplied.

"Great. Then let's get ours to go. Game?" he offered her his hand.

Hesitating the briefest of seconds, Estelle smiled. "Game." She placed her fingers in his. "See you two," she said gaily, and hand in hand they went to the order counter.

"Methinks we've been had, Mary Theresa," Nelson said evenly when the pair left without a backward glance, carrying their treats out to Jonathan's car.

She had the same impression herself, but couldn't express it as eloquently.

"Hungry?" he asked.

Mary shook her head.

"Me, neither. I could go for a soda, though. How about you?"

"Sure. Soda I like, too." But she couldn't help wishing she had her hands around her friend's slender little neck. That girl had to be the rudest, most brazen, downright— She couldn't even think of an English word to fit.

Flagging down the young waitress, Nelson placed their order, and she brought the drinks over almost immediately.

"Well," he said after taking a long draught through his straw, "my sister appears to have finally decided to give good buddy Jon a tumble. It's about time, really. She's been mooning over her dead fiancé long enough." A slow grin widened his mouth, and he raked fingers through his reddish-brown hair, leaving paths among the shiny strands. "Poor old Jon's been carrying a torch for her since high school."

"Good together they look," Mary had to admit, smiling. Then she sensed Nelson's gaze searching her face. There seemed to be some quality in his eyes she'd never noticed before. . .and she couldn't afford to find out what it was. Neither could she afford to reveal her own feelings. That was the absolute last thing she needed right now. She lowered her eyelids and gave her full concentration to her soda. The time had come to make arrangements to move to Florida. She'd do it as soon as possible. Sooner.

But first things first. Tomorrow, when she saw Estelle at work, she would throttle her.

Nelson leaned closer. "How's your drink?"

nineteen

Aware that Nelson had finished his soda, Mary Theresa quickly gulped hers down, then blotted her lips on the paper napkin.

"Ready to go?"

She nodded. "Thank you for buying me drink."

"Anytime." They rose, and he allowed her to precede him. Reaching around to push open the door, he then walked her to the car.

So wonderfully attentive. Too much so. She would remember this always.

Still, Mary couldn't help her relief that the evening would soon end. She did appreciate its beauty, with the first stars appearing in the darkening sky, the mild summer breeze. It would provide precious memories to look back on someday, when she could bear to. For now, she would just pretend tonight was like any other, with her heading home from supper at Estelle's. Yet how could she completely ignore the fact she was with Nelson, or the incredible peace which filled her heart? The peace, at least, was hers to keep. God loved and accepted her, exactly as she was, and He'd gifted her with an extra few sweet moments alone with Nelson. . .entirely unplanned and more than she'd dared to dream.

Neither spoke as they reached the car. Nelson handed her inside, closed the door, and went around to his side. He started the motor and pulled away from the curb. But he didn't turn in the direction of her apartment.

Mary felt a twinge of panic and sent him a questioning look.

"Thought we might take a little drive," he said. "Seems a shame to waste such a pretty night."

Well, okay, I can do this, she assured herself. *He is the one who gave me the Bible, knelt with me in prayer. I can trust him. And I will have another memory to cherish. A few moments more.* The city did look lovely, with subdued lights here and there inside the tall buildings, a sprinkling of colored neon signs at gas stations and diners. She tried to concentrate on those things.

"Feel like walking a bit?" Nelson asked casually as they neared Central Park. "Just because I can drive now, doesn't mean I want to revert to sitting around all the time."

"Maybe a short walk," she replied. "Work is tomorrow."

"Sure, I understand. I'm a working man myself now." He pulled into one of the main drives, found a spot to park, then got out and came around to assist her.

He couldn't have chosen a more perfect night, Mary decided, inhaling the fragrant perfumes of the late summer plants as they strolled along one of the walkways. Black-purple fruit of the elderberry glistened from nearby lights, and she could easily imagine the glory of all the chrysanthemums in the sunshine. The whole world seemed brand-new, somehow, and she appreciated God's handiwork in an entirely different way.

Just beyond a wooden footbridge, they came to an open pavilion, dim but illuminated by standing lights positioned around the grounds. They mounted the steps to the circular stage. Hands in his pockets, Nelson gazed over the well-kept greenery and shrubs surrounding them. "I used to come here pretty often. That is, my family did. For the outdoor concerts. People would bring chairs or blankets, and we'd sit and bask in the music of the big bands. It was great. Maybe they still give concerts, who knows?"

Mary leaned back against the railing, admiring the twinkling stars against a blue velvet sky as he talked. She loved the way Nelson's voice sang across her heartstrings, and if he wanted to stand there forever and talk, she'd be content to listen that long.

A few moments of silence passed before he emitted a silent chuckle and turned to her. "You know, lately I was starting to think you were avoiding us. Or to be more precise, avoiding me."

The fine hairs on her arms prickled, and the breeze suddenly felt chilly.

"Was I wrong?"

Mary could find no reason to hide the truth. He'd find out soon enough, anyway. She lowered her gaze and shook her head.

"So, which was it then? The family or me?"

"Both."

He released a sudden rush of breath, and his shoulders flattened.

"But not for reason you think," she elaborated.

"You mean, we didn't do anything to offend you then."

"No. Never. Very. . .loving is your family." *Too loving. I love all of you too much.*

"That doesn't make a whole lot of sense, Mary," he said, a frown creasing his forehead. "If you're happy around us, why would you feel you needed to avoid us?"

"Be–because too close I am getting." She paused. "Away. I must go away. To Florida."

"To visit someone?"

She shook her head. "To live. Soon. Before too hard it is."

"Well, that's a relief," he blurted sarcastically, raising a hand and letting it fall to his side. His droll tone indicated an attempt to lighten the moment. "I thought maybe you were uncomfortable being around my. . .injury. Women generally don't flock around a guy like me, you might say."

"The injury? No. To me this is not important," she answered

in all honesty. "A man like you many girls would want."

"Would you?" He locked his gaze on hers.

Mary's heart thudded to a stop. She had to look away.

He stepped closer, placing his hands on her shoulders. "Because I might as well level with you, Mary Theresa. I lov—"

"No!" Mary gasped, pressing her fingertips to his lips. An inexpressible ache crushed her spirit, and her broken heart throbbed so, she wondered if he felt the pulse in her touch. Tears welled up inside, but she suppressed them by sheer force of will. She had to hold herself together a little while longer. She would have the rest of her life to cry. "You must not say that," she whispered. "Not to me. Never to me." She tried to ease out of his grip.

But Nelson only held tighter, confusion etching his finely honed features. "Don't be ridiculous. Why shouldn't I say that to the woman I want to marry?"

To marry. Mary had relinquished that dream long ago. It was far too late to consider something so utterly hopeless. Her head drooped in defeat. "Reasons are. . .too many."

A ragged breath issued from him. "Name one."

She searched his face in the subdued light, hating the pain she saw there, hating that she was the cause. . .and most of all, hating that if she did tell him her reasons, she would inflict even more hurt. The crushing weight of the words she knew she would have to say to him almost suffocated her.

But it was the only sure way to make him understand.

Father, please give me the strength I need to do this. Mustering every ounce of fortitude she possessed, she steeled herself against the love for Nelson which had been growing inside her from the moment they'd met. She tugged herself forcefully from his grasp and turned away a little, to avoid having to witness the brutal blow she had no other choice but to administer. She would never be able to live with herself if she watched the effects of her confession. *Just take me home,* her heart begged. *Let us leave now. Please. I cannot do this. I cannot.*

But he stood there, feet planted, not moving. Waiting.

The rate of Mary's heart intensified until it throbbed in her ears, each beat a death knoll to her relationship with Nelson Thomas. She could feel the pounding in her neck, could feel the heat rising to her face. It seemed a struggle even to breathe, to swallow. "Like others I am not," she finally choked out. "Not like Estelle, not like woman you should marry."

"What are you saying?" he probed.

A dark pain clutched her heart, filling her throat. How could she speak the words? How could she dredge up the horrific memories which could take years to banish completely from her thoughts and nightmares? Even as the battle raged within her, Mary chanced a tiny look—a last look—at the only man she had ever loved. The man who had led her to the Lord and helped her to trust again. This man of whom she was not worthy, could never be worthy.

How can I not tell him?

She drew a shuddering breath and plunged ahead, before her love for him could make her change her mind. "In Ravensbruck, in death camp," she heard herself whisper, "I was. . . *comfort girl,* for German officers. M—many officers. They—"

"Stop! Stop!" Nelson shrank back several inches, his head shaking in refusal, his jawline hardening. Mary sensed his eyes piercing her very soul.

Renewed loathing for herself and those faceless beasts in uniform flowed through Mary like vomit, withering her heart. It hadn't been worth it, to survive. She should have refused. Fought. Let them gas her. Death would have been better than having to endure this.

A sound issued from the depths of Nelson's being that was not human. A sound Mary Theresa had heard often during her confinement, from prisoners whose loved ones were tortured and murdered before their eyes. It would haunt her as long as she lived. On the edge of her vision, she saw his head sag into his hands, and his broad shoulders began to shake.

This time, *he* turned from *her.*

Her heart dropped within her with a sickening thud. Only the things she had survived before enabled her to live through his shuddering sobs. She blinked back the tears trembling on her eyelashes.

She'd known from the beginning that the two of them could never become involved. That when he went, so would his family. . .including Estelle. She should not have cultivated those friendships, yet she could not help herself. They had shown her the love she'd been so hungry for. And she'd needed it so.

"To tell you I did not want. You make me tell," she lamented, knowing it didn't matter. Nothing mattered now. "I knew you would hate me. I. . .I am going now."

He swung back, his face ravaged with tears. "Hate you?" he asked incredulously. *"Hate you?"*

Mary swallowed, trying to think of what could be worse, what degree of contempt lay beyond even hatred.

Nelson swiped the wetness from his face. And with the tenderest smile she had ever seen, he reached for her and drew her close, crushing her to his chest, rocking her in his strong arms. "I could never hate you, Mary Theresa," he murmured huskily against her hair. "Never. I love you more than life itself. Those months at the death camp, those. . .terrible things you endured. . .none of that was your fault, your doing. It was all done *to* you. You had no choice. You were the victim. If I abhor anybody," he grated, "it's those animals that could do such deplorable, inexcusable, inhumane things to an angel like you. But I can only leave their ultimate judgment to God."

Closing her eyes against an exquisite pain cinching itself

around her heart, Mary still doubted the words she'd never dreamed she'd hear in her lifetime.

"Both of us were victims of war, my love," he went on. "Things were done to us that we had no control over. But it's time to let go of the past and forgive those who caused our suffering. Only then will our healing be complete."

Mary had not prepared herself for this. She'd braced herself for his utter disgust, for his ultimate rejection. She'd expected Nelson to turn his back and walk out of her life forever. But, this! This was the unconditional kind of love Corrie ten Boom had spoken of. The kind of love God had for the people who repented of their sins and accepted His Son. "Y–you still love me? Even now?"

The realization completely shattered the floodgates behind her eyes.

With a strangled sob, Mary sought Nelson's comfort, losing herself in those strong arms. Burying her face in his solid chest, she wept for the first time since she'd been taken into captivity. Great, huge sobs for herself, for her relatives, for the torment and shame of her past, for losses which could never be recovered.

On the fringes of her consciousness, she felt him scoop her up into his arms and cradle her there like a child. He eased down to the banister and sat stroking her back, her hair, making no move to stem the cleansing tide, as if he sensed her need to relinquish those hurtful memories once and for all.

Mary relaxed a little in his embrace, then a little more, drawing comfort and sustenance from that stalwart heart beating against her own. Slowly, gradually, the chains that had bound her for so long melted away. Her slowing tears took a new turn, becoming a wellspring of joy over the new life she had found in the Lord, with the Thomases, and best of all, with Nelson. No matter what the future held for them, it would never seem as hopeless as before. Because of him. Because of God.

At last, she fell silent.

Nelson continued to hold her closely, rocking her tenderly, his wordless solace infusing her with even more peace and hope. Then he gently set her to her feet and stood facing her. With the edge of his index finger, he raised her chin and looked deep into her soul. "My dearest Mary, don't ever hang that lovely head again. You became a new creation earlier this evening. Old things are passed away, and all things are become new. God has erased your past and made you pure in His Son. He's given you an inner beauty that radiates from your eyes and shines out at me whenever I look at you, a beauty even beyond your outward appearance." His thumbs brushed away the last traces of tears from her face, and he smiled into her soul. "And I'm asking you to stay. Please. Don't go away. Because if you'd deign to consider a guy with a bit of a limp, I'd be honored to have you for my wife."

He still wanted her! Despite everything! Her lips curved into a tremulous smile. She tested her voice, surprised to hear it when it came out. "For a long time, I am loving you, Nelson. The honor is mine. I will stay."

"I'm glad you said that," he breathed, the circle of his arms tightening around her. "Oh, Mary, nothing in this world will ever hurt you again. This I promise with all my heart." Lowering his head, he covered her lips with his, in a kiss that said far more than mere words ever could.

Mary snuggled closer as he deepened the kiss. *Thank You, dear God,* her heart sang, *for teaching me forgiveness, for giving me love.* Despite those old feelings of unworthiness, her past no longer mattered. The Lord had graciously given her far more than the desires of her heart, and she didn't know how to begin expressing her praises.

"Come on, my angel," Nelson crooned, hugging her to his

side. "I know a few people who're gonna want to hear about this. And on the way, we can start making some plans."

And the two of them stepped out into the beautiful night.

epilogue

A few late-falling snowflakes danced on the wind beneath a sky of clearest blue, adding even more frosty glory to a city blanketed in white. Peering out at the beauty from the lace curtains on Estelle's bedroom windows, Mary could hardly speak. Everything looked so pure, so pristine. . .just the way she felt.

"Stand straight," her friend coaxed, "or I'll never get these pearl buttons fastened."

Doing her bidding, Mary gazed down at the lovely bridal gown Mrs. Thomas had poured all her love into making. Of purest white satin, with long lacy sleeves and a bodice trimmed with seed pearls and sparkles, she felt like a princess.

Stunning in her own radiance, Rahel stepped close enough to give her a mute but fiercely emotional hug. "*Kocham Ciebie*, I love you," she whispered, her deep brown eyes shining with moisture. Her long, dark hair and olive complexion glowed against a rich emerald gown with a complementing headpiece of satin and tulle. "Fortunate you are. Be happy." Having come expressly to stand up for Mary, she was quickly forming an attachment to the rest of the family and would find it hard to return to her solitary life in Florida. . .if she could bring herself to leave at all.

"Now for your veil," Estelle said, misty-eyed as she stood by in a gown identical to Rahel's, her shining curls even more glorious next to the fabric's deep color. Picking up the beaded Juliet cap and veil her mom had fashioned, she set it in place and pinned it to Mary's hair, unfolding the blusher veil over her face.

Mom Thomas rapped on the door, then opened it to peek around, her cheeks pink against a deep wine-colored suit. "Oh, my pretty girls," she murmured, all teary and flustered. "I couldn't be more proud of you." Crossing to them, she gave all three a hug, unconcerned about crushing the satin and taffeta creations she'd labored over. "Everything's ready downstairs for our Christmas wedding. Let's get your flowers." She bustled to the florist's box on Estelle's bed to pass out bouquets of red carnations and white roses whose fragrance filled the room.

Estelle stood back to admire Mary, then gave her a hug, also. "Now you'll be my real sister, you know. I've never been so happy."

"I, too," she whispered, unable to trust her voice.

Piano music drifted from downstairs in prelude to "The Wedding March," and her soon-to-be father-in-law appeared and offered his elbow. "You look lovely," he assured her. "Let's not keep poor Nelson waiting any longer."

The scent of pine drifted upstairs from the long-needled evergreen the family had decorated last night. Large poinsettia plants lifted brilliant faces from several spots throughout the downstairs, lending an even more festive air, as did the tall red candles burning so brightly on the mantel. One by one, the women started their measured descent down the stairs whose railings sported red velvet bows and holly.

Mary, trailing a few steps behind, reached the landing, her hand on Dad Thomas's black-suited arm.

Her gaze immediately sought Nelson's and almost melted from the depth of love and admiration she saw in his light brown eyes. In his new charcoal pinstripe, he looked tall and resplendent, standing beside the lovely Christmas tree hung with tinsel and shining ornaments. She couldn't help believing she was getting the better end of things. . .not only in her betrothed's masculine appearance but in his spiritual maturity, which would benefit her throughout their life together.

As the traditional wedding piece rang out, Mary smiled and started toward the man who, by example, had demonstrated God's forgiveness and love, making her whole again.

Never once taking his eyes from her, Nelson smiled and stepped to her side, enfolding her hand in his with a reassuring squeeze. Then, together, they turned to face the minister.

A Letter To Our Readers

Dear Reader:

In order that we might better contribute to your reading enjoyment, we would appreciate your taking a few minutes to respond to the following questions. We welcome your comments and read each form and letter we receive. When completed, please return to the following:

Rebecca Germany, Fiction Editor
Heartsong Presents
PO Box 719
Uhrichsville, Ohio 44683

1. Did you enjoy reading *Remnant of Forgiveness* by Sally Laity?

    ❏ Very much! I would like to see more books by this author!

    ❏ Moderately. I would have enjoyed it more if

_____

_____

2. Are you a member of **Heartsong Presents**? Yes ❏ No ❏
   If no, where did you purchase this book?_____

_____

3. How would you rate, on a scale from 1 (poor) to 5 (superior), the cover design?_____

4. On a scale from 1 (poor) to 10 (superior), please rate the following elements.

_____ Heroine   _____ Plot

_____ Hero   _____ Inspirational theme

_____ Setting   _____ Secondary characters

5. These characters were special because_____
   _____
   _____

6. How has this book inspired your life?_____
   _____
   _____

7. What settings would you like to see covered in future
   Heartsong Presents books?_____
   _____
   _____

8. What are some inspirational themes you would like to see
   treated in future books?_____
   _____
   _____

9. Would you be interested in reading other **Heartsong
   Presents** titles?   Yes ☐   No ☐

10. Please check your age range:
    ☐ Under 18   ☐ 18-24   ☐ 25-34
    ☐ 35-45   ☐ 46-55   ☐ Over 55

11. How many hours per week do you read?_____

Name _____

Occupation _____

Address _____

City _____ State _____ Zip _____

Heirloom Brides

*L*ove and faith are the greatest of inheritances.

These four closely related stories will warm your heart with family love and traditions. Each bride has a legacy of faith to leave with generations to come. And the heirloom chest will forever be symbolic of their love.

paperback, 464 pages, 5 ³/₁₆" x 8"

❤ • ❤ • ❤ • ❤ • ❤ • ❤ • ❤ • ❤ • ❤ • ❤

❤ • ❤ • ❤ • ❤ • ❤ • ❤ • ❤ • ❤ • ❤ • ❤

·····Hearts♥ng·····

HISTORICAL ROMANCE IS CHEAPER BY THE DOZEN!

Buy any assortment of twelve *Heartsong Presents* titles and save 25% off of the already discounted price of $2.95 each!

Any 12 *Heartsong Presents* titles for only $26.95 *

*plus $1.00 shipping and handling per order and sales tax where applicable.

HEARTSONG PRESENTS TITLES AVAILABLE NOW:

__HP111 A KINGDOM DIVIDED, T. Peterson
__HP179 HER FATHER'S LOVE, N. Lavo
__HP183 A NEW LOVE, V. Wiggins
__HP184 THE HOPE THAT SINGS, J. A. Grote
__HP196 DREAMS FULFILLED, L. Herring
__HP200 IF ONLY, T. Peterson
__HP203 AMPLE PORTIONS, D. L. Christner
__HP207 THE EAGLE AND THE LAMB, D. Mindrup
__HP208 LOVE'S TENDER PATH, B. L. Etchison
__HP211 MY VALENTINE, T. Peterson
__HP215 TULSA TRESPASS, N. J. Lutz
__HP219 A HEART FOR HOME, N. Morris
__HP220 SONG OF THE DOVE, P. Darty
__HP223 THREADS OF LOVE, J. M. Miller
__HP224 EDGE OF DESTINY, D. Mindrup
__HP227 BRIDGET'S BARGAIN, L. Lough
__HP228 FALLING WATER VALLEY, M. L. Colln
__HP235 THE LADY ROSE, J. Williams
__HP236 VALIANT HEART, S. Laity
__HP239 LOGAN'S LADY, T. Peterson
__HP240 THE SUN STILL SHINES, L. Ford
__HP243 THE RISING SON, D. Mindrup
__HP247 STRONG AS THE REDWOOD, K. Billerbeck
__HP248 RETURN TO TULSA, N. J. Lutz
__HP251 ESCAPE ON THE WIND, J. LaMunyon
__HP256 THE PROMISE OF RAIN, S. Krueger
__HP259 FIVE GEESE FLYING, T. Peterson
__HP260 THE WILL AND THE WAY, D. Pace
__HP263 THE STARFIRE QUILT, A. Allen
__HP264 JOURNEY TOWARD HOME, C. Cox

__HP267 FOR A SONG, K. Scarth
__HP268 UNCHAINED HEARTS, L. Ford
__HP271 WHERE LEADS THE HEART, C. Coble
__HP272 ALBERT'S DESTINY, B. L. Etchison
__HP275 ALONG UNFAMILIAR PATHS, A. Rognlie
__HP276 THE MOUNTAIN'S SON, G. Brandt
__HP279 AN UNEXPECTED LOVE, A. Boeshaar
__HP280 A LIGHT WITHIN, D. Mindrup
__HP283 IN LIZZY'S IMAGE, C. R. Scheidies
__HP284 TEXAS HONOR, D. W. Smith
__HP291 REHOBOTH, D. Mills
__HP292 A CHILD OF PROMISE, J. Stengl
__HP295 TEND THE LIGHT, S. Hayden
__HP296 ONCE MORE CHANCE, K. Comeaux
__HP299 EM'S ONLY CHANCE, R. Dow
__HP300 CHANGES OF THE HEART, J. M. Miller
__HP303 MAID OF HONOR, C. R. Scheidies
__HP304 SONG OF THE CIMARRON, K. R. Stevens
__HP307 SILENT STRANGER, P. Darty
__HP308 A DIFFERENT KIND OF HEAVEN, T. Shuttlesworth
__HP311 IF THE PROSPECT PLEASES, S. Laity
__HP312 OUT OF THE DARKNESS, D. Crawford and R. Druten
__HP315 MY ENEMY, MY LOVE, D. Mindrup
__HP319 MARGARET'S QUEST, M. Chapman
__HP320 HOPE IN THE GREAT SOUTHLAND, M. Hawkins
__HP323 NO MORE SEA, G. Brandt
__HP324 LOVE IN THE GREAT SOUTHLAND, M. Hawkins
__HP327 PLAINS OF PROMISE, C. Coble
__HP328 STRANGER'S BRIDE, D. Hunter
__HP331 A MAN FOR LIBBY, J. A. Grote

(If ordering from this page, please remember to include it with the order form.)

Hearts♥ng Presents
Love Stories Are Rated G!

That's for godly, gratifying, and of course, great! If you love a thrilling love story, but don't appreciate the sordidness of some popular paperback romances, **Heartsong Presents** is for you. In fact, **Heartsong Presents** is the *only inspirational romance book club* featuring love stories where Christian faith is the primary ingredient in a marriage relationship.

Sign up today to receive your first set of four, never before published Christian romances. Send no money now; you will receive a bill with the first shipment. You may cancel at any time without obligation, and if you aren't completely satisfied with any selection, you may return the books for an immediate refund!

Imagine. . .four new romances every four weeks—two historical, two contemporary—with men and women like you who long to meet the one God has chosen as the love of their lives. . . all for the low price of $9.97 postpaid.

To join, simply complete the coupon below and mail to the address provided. **Heartsong Presents** romances are rated G for another reason: They'll arrive *Godspeed!*